*A
Harlequin
Romance*

ALIEN CORN

by

RACHEL LINDSAY

HARLEQUIN BOOKS   TORONTO
WINNIPEG

Original hard cover edition published in 1968
by Mills & Boon Limited.

© Scribe Associates Limited 1968

SBN 373-01742-1

Harlequin edition published December 1973

Printed in Canada

CHAPTER ONE

Lorna Fairfax hurried through the lounge of the Hyde Park Palace Hotel and gave the revolving doors an angry push. They whirled round and a young woman about to step in was thrown violently into her arms.

'I'm sorry,' she began, and then stopped. 'Amalia — it can't be!'

'Lorna! Of all the people in the world fancy bumping into you! Don't tell me you're staying here too?'

Lorna grinned. 'Not likely! I only work here.'

'Then I'm in luck. I've been trying to get you on the telephone all day. But we can't stand talking here. Come inside and have tea.'

Momentarily Lorna hesitated. She had already broken one rule by coming out through the front entrance and it might cost her her job to be seen sitting with a visitor.

As if guessing her thoughts the other girl smiled. 'Come on, Lorna. You can always tell the manager I wouldn't take no for an answer!'

With a shrug Lorna followed her friend across the carpeted foyer to a corner of the peach-mirrored lounge.

'How long have you been here, Amalia? I haven't seen your name in the register.'

'You wouldn't recognize it if you did. I'm married!'

'Impossible! You still look such a kid!'

'That's what Manoel says. Oh, Lorna, it *is* good to see you. You haven't changed a bit.'

'Neither have you.'

And indeed she had not: the same bubbly hair, curly mouth and twinkling dark eyes. The only difference was that the brown gymslip had been replaced by a smartly cut grey suit and the small, expressive hands sported an outsize diamond ring. Amalia had obviously married well.

'Now then, where shall we begin?' The Portuguese girl turned back from the waiter. 'Such a lot has happened since I last saw you. How are your parents and that lovely house? Do you still live with them in the country?'

Regretfully Lorna remembered the gracious Queen Anne house, the beech woods and sloping lawns that had been her background as a child.

'Finished,' she said briefly. 'My parents died soon after my brother John was killed, and I had to sell up the house and move in with an aunt.'

'Lorna dear, I never knew – never guessed. Why didn't you write and tell me?'

'How could I? We'd lost touch ages before. Now don't look so miserable, there's no need to be. I've a lovely little flat in Chelsea and quite a bit of the family silver! But enough about me. What are *you* doing here? Are you staying long?'

'A few days. As a matter of fact I've been living in Brazil since I got married. Manoel looks after his cousin's estate out there and we're on our way to Portugal for a holiday.'

'Perhaps you'll come over to the flat one evening. If not now, on your return.'

Amalia's lips curled in a smile. 'We won't be returning until the end of the year, and when we do there'll be three of us!'

'Amalia, how wonderful – I'd never have guessed! Is that the reason you're going back to Portugal?'

'Yes. Rafael – that's the cousin I was telling you about – wants the baby to be born in the family home.'

'Quite the patriarch!'

Amalia shrugged. 'He's been very good to us since our marriage, and we wouldn't oppose him.'

'And your parents – where are they?'

'At the Embassy in Rio, worse luck. That was one of

the reasons I didn't want to come back.' She poured out the tea and passed Lorna a cup. 'It's a pity you don't live nearer or you could come and keep me company! Manoel's relations are as old as the Ark, and after Rio, Estoril will be as dull as ditch-water.' She sat up. 'But of course! Why didn't I think of it before? It's the ideal solution! You must come and stay with me until I've had the baby!'

Lorna smiled. 'It sounds wonderful, but I couldn't.'

'Why? Are you engaged?'

'No, but—'

'Well, what's stopping you? Silly Lorna, I'm not asking you out of pity. I'm offering you a job. Manoel will fix a salary and—'

'Amalia, no! I wouldn't dream of taking any money from you. If I came at all it would be as a friend.' She hesitated. 'I'm really thinking of my aunt. We took the flat together and it doesn't seem right to leave her on her own.'

'I don't see why. You wouldn't be away for ever. Please, Lorna, you can't refuse without thinking it over. You know as well as I do I've nothing in common with Portuguese girls of my own age. If I don't have someone like you to talk to I'll go—' she stopped and waved frantically to a man walking towards the lift. He turned and came over with a smile.

Not very tall, slender, with the sleek black hair and expressive eyes of his race, this was obviously Manoel. Happily Amalia introduced them and he watched her fondly as she prattled on about Lorna's visit to Portugal.

'Amalia, my love,' he interrupted the flow, 'you have not given your friend a chance to say a word.' Then to Lorna: 'What's all this about your coming to Portugal? I think it would be an excellent idea. My wife needs someone to cheer her up.'

'It isn't settled, I'm afraid. I've promised to let Amalia know tomorrow, Senhor—'

'Rodriguez. Manoel Rodriguez at your service.'

Solemnly they shook hands all over again and Lorna rose. 'I really must be going this time or my aunt will think I'm lost.'

'Telephone me early,' Amalia pleaded, 'I'll be keeping my fingers crossed until I hear from you.'

As Lorna had expected, her aunt was delighted when she heard the reason for her niece's delay.

'It's just the sort of thing you've been looking for. You're going, of course?'

'I said I'd think it over.'

'Think it over? My dear girl, you'd be mad to refuse. It isn't as if you'd be leaving a wonderful job or a hectic social life. There's nothing to stop you going. You're in a rut and this is the best way of getting out of it.'

'Now don't *you* say I look as if I need a holiday or I'll really feel decrepit!'

Lorna took off her coat and looked at herself in the mirror. Her heart-shaped face with its wide-spaced grey eyes and gentle mouth was completely devoid of make-up, the skin milky-white except for a faint flush on the high cheekbones. Soft, ash-blonde hair was pulled back into a tight knot without any concession to style; the same disregard of fashion evident in the shapeless wool dress that covered her tall, slim body.

'What's the matter with me?' she asked. 'I'm young, not repulsive to look at, yet life seems to be passing me by.'

'Because you've let yourself go,' her aunt said tartly. 'I've never known a girl of your age take so little interest in herself. If you stopped trying to improve your mind and concentrated a bit more on your appearance you wouldn't be sitting at home so much. There's nothing wrong with you that a young man can't put right!'

Lorna laughed. 'And how am I supposed to find this Romeo?'

'Not in the past – I can tell you that! It's no good pining for the country, my dear. When you sold your home that part of your life ended for ever. I don't know why Derek puts up with you. He's crazy to bother with someone who takes as little notice of him as you do.'

Lorna sat down and picked up her knitting, the flying needles the only outward sign of disturbance. 'Derek's a dear, but I don't love him.'

'If that's the case there's no more to say. But don't throw away a decent boy for the sake of an unknown knight in shining armour.' Her aunt leaned forward earnestly. 'I'd take your friend's offer, Lorna. If you're worrying about the fare . . .'

'Of course not, but—'

'What's stopping you, then? If you're thinking about me – don't. I'll miss you – I won't deny that – but at least it'll give me a chance to write a lot more. No evening meals to cook and I can live on tea and buns until you get back!'

'If I didn't know you, I'd think you were trying to get rid of me!' Lorna stood up and yawned. 'All right, I'll sleep on it and decide in the morning.'

But her decision was already made; it had only needed her aunt to confirm it. Early the next day she telephoned her friend and said she would accept the offer. Amalia was delighted.

'I'm sure you won't regret it. Oh, Lorna, it'll be like old times, I can't wait until we're together again! Manoel and I will pick you up on Wednesday on the way to the airport.'

'It's impossible – I'll never be ready by then! I've got so much to do I'll be lucky if I can leave in a month.'

'Don't worry about the visa. A cousin of Manoel's works at the Portuguese Legation and he'll get you one in a few hours.'

'I need more than a visa to get out of England,' Lorna

said wryly. 'I haven't got a passport yet – and no cousin in the world can expedite the Foreign Office!'

'Can't you explain you're in a hurry?'

'It wouldn't do any good. And honestly, Amalia, even if my passport came through tomorrow I couldn't just pack up and leave. For one thing I haven't any clothes and for another I've got to give in my notice.'

'Bother your notice! The manager can't stop you from leaving.'

'No, but he can give me a bad reference.'

'Well, I'll give you a good one!' Amalia's voice quickened. 'I can't talk any more. Manoel and I are going out for the day and he's signalling me to hurry. I'll telephone you this evening if I don't get back too late.'

Because of her conversation with Amalia, Lorna was late arriving at the hotel and had hardly settled down at her desk when she was called to the manager's office. Mystified at the summons – for Mr. Irving rarely saw the lesser members of his staff – she hurried along the corridor and entered the large, close-carpeted room.

Mr. Irving took off his silver-rimmed glasses and polished them slowly as he spoke. 'I've had a complaint about you, Miss Fairfax. Surely you have been here long enough to know it is against the rules for the staff to use the main exits.'

'I'm sorry, sir, but I – I forgot.'

'And did you also forget that it is against the rules for employees to have tea in the main lounge?'

'Senhora Rodriguez invited me and I couldn't refuse. She is an old school friend of mine.'

'I see.' The manager fingered his chin, his expression indicative of his annoyance at discovering that one of his employees should dare to know a hotel guest. 'I realize that you are in an awkward position, Miss Fairfax, but then so am I. I cannot show favouritism to anyone, and I must insist that in future you meet your friend outside the hotel. Our rules cannot be waived for one person. If you disregard them I shall have no alternative but to ask you to leave.'

'There's no need to do that, Mr. Irving. I would rather lose my job than offend Senhora Rodriguez. I've worked here quite a few years and always thought you were pleased with me.'

'I'm not complaining of your work, Miss Fairfax.'

'I know, but if you can consider giving me notice for such a small thing it's obvious you've never appreciated my work.'

'The question of appreciation doesn't enter into it. You are paid to do your job well and—'

'There are certain things you can't pay for.'

'Such as?'

'Loyalty and trust.'

She was at the door when he called after her, 'I hope *you* appreciate that you are throwing away a good job. If you care to reconsider it . . .'

'No, thank you, Mr. Irving.'

'In that case it would be as well if you left at the end of the week.'

For the next fortnight Lorna's days were filled with visits to Caxton Hall for her passport forms, calling at the Portuguese Legation for her visa, and queueing up at Cook's to collect her traveller's cheques and book her passage to Portugal.

Derek was the only one of her friends who did not enthuse over her forthcoming departure, and although he said nothing to discourage her from going, his increased attention made her realize that her aunt had been right about him.

On the Saturday before she was due to leave they dined together at a little country inn on the Thames, and watching the swans glide gracefully along the water she wondered if any other scenes she might see on her journey abroad could compete with this one for beauty and tranquillity.

'Why the sigh, Lorna?' Derek asked quietly.

'I don't know. Cold feet, perhaps, and the fear that I might be homesick.'

'You won't be away long enough for that.'

'At least six months. Perhaps even longer.'

'I hope not.' He caught her hand. 'It's bad enough to know I won't be seeing you all the summer without having to face the thought of a London winter without you!' She laughed and he shook his head. 'I didn't mean it as a joke. I'm serious, Lorna, surely you know that? I've not spoken about my feelings before because I didn't think you cared, but I can't let you go hundreds of miles away and not tell you I love you.' He paused. 'I'm putting this awfully badly, but you can blame yourself — when I'm with you I can't even think straight. What I'm trying to say is that I love you and want to marry you.'

Lorna pulled her hand away from his and wished wholeheartedly that she had never agreed to come out alone with him tonight. Nothing was more embarrassing than to be the recipient of an unwanted proposal, yet at the same time she would not have been human if she did not feel a tiny thrill at receiving her first offer of marriage. Nervously she pushed back a strand of hair.

'I don't know what to say, Derek. It's come as such a surprise.'

'But you must have known!'

'I knew you liked me, but I never thought in that way.'

'In what other way, then? As a sister?'

She smiled slightly. 'I wasn't going to say anything as trite as that. But you must admit you never gave me any inkling you were in love with me.'

'Because I was afraid of rushing you. I wouldn't have said anything now, except that I couldn't bear the thought of your going away and leaving things in the air between us.' He leaned across the table. 'Please, darling, say you'll marry me.'

'I can't! I – I wish I could. But there's so much of the

world I haven't seen, so many things I want to do before I settle down. Oh, Derek, don't look so miserable. I don't want to hurt you.'

'You can't expect me to look delighted at what you've just said. Damn it, Lorna, I'm only flesh and blood!'

She bit her lip. 'If I were in love with you it would be so simple.'

'If you were in love with me, you wouldn't be going!' With an effort he forced himself to smile. 'Now let's forget what I've said and enjoy the evening.'

It was a damp, drizzly Monday morning when Lorna left London Airport. Although it was her first flight she soon grew accustomed to the strangeness of travelling high above the earth, and looking out through the window saw only the grey, filmy cloud that shrouded them for most of the journey. But it was a clear, sunny afternoon five hours later when the silver airliner touched down on the tarmac of Lisbon Airport. The sky was brilliantly blue, but a fierce wind tugged at her skirt, and holding her hat firmly with her hand she ran the last few yards to the shelter of the Customs shed.

She had telegraphed Amalia the time of her arrival, but her friend was not amongst the people milling in the main office.

'Mees Fairfax?' A plump official stood before her and Lorna nodded. 'Senhor Rodriguez sends a thousand apologies. Anozer business keep him from meeting you, but he send his car instead.'

With a low bow and an eloquent wave of the hand he escorted her into a gleaming, chauffeur-driven Cadillac. One certainly had to hand it to the Latin countries for courtesy, Lorna thought, as they drew away from the kerb. Even his atrocious English had not prevented the little man from conveying a wish to please, and she suppressed a desire to peep out through the rear window and see if he was still bowing the car out of sight.

Within an hour of leaving the airport they were at
Estoril, and Lorna was enchanted with her first sight of
the seaside town. A miniature fortress was silhouetted on
a cliff in the distance and a row of palm trees edged the
esplanade that overlooked the beach. She had no more
than a brief glimpse of the sea breaking into white spume
on the sands before the car skirted the bulk of the Palace
Hotel, nosed its way past the private houses that lay on a
gentle incline and turned in at a pair of wrought iron
gates.

They bowled along a drive bordered with flowering
shrubs towards a long, low house, its pink-washed walls
and green shuttered windows giving it an air of gaiety
and lightness. A wide terrace ran its length and three
steps in the centre led up to an oak-studded door.

The car stopped and before Lorna could get out
Amalia was running down to greet her.

'Lorna, how lovely to see you! I'm sorry I couldn't
meet you at the airport, but Manoel promised to come
back for me and in the end he wasn't able to.'

Together they walked up the steps into the house and
Lorna stared at the hall in wonder. Octagonal in shape,
stone arches with built-in doors ran along its eight sides,
giving it a cathedral-like quality heightened by the
stained glass window in the dome-shaped roof. Large
urns filled with flowering shrubs stood against the wall
and bright rugs patterned the floor, their motif repeated
on the carpet that covered the curving stairs.

Amalia gave her no chance to pause and preceded her
up the stairs to a room at the far end of a narrow corridor.

'I'm sorry I couldn't give you a bedroom overlooking
the sea, but there are only two – one is Rafael's and the
other his mother's.'

'I didn't expect it,' Lorna said quickly. 'This one is
ideal.'

'Good. I'll just make sure Luiz is bringing up your cases,
then you can tidy up and come downstairs for tea.'

Left alone, Lorna walked to the window and looked down on the garden, still admiring the view when Luiz entered with her bags. The furniture was white and gold, in Regency period, the bedspread and pelmets in striped blue and gold satin. Humming softly to herself, she tidied up and hurried along the corridor, brought up short as her feet threatened to slip on the highly polished floors.

Downstairs again she hesitated. The archways were so alike that it was difficult to decide which one led to the drawing-room, and it was a relief when Amalia appeared at one of the doors.

'I guessed you'd be stuck here – most of our guests are! Come and have tea and then I'll take you to meet my aunt.'

The *sala* or main room was one of the loveliest Lorna had ever seen. Two long settees and numerous high-backed easy chairs were patterned in the same gold tapestry as the curtains at the long windows. Hand-made rugs on the dark wooden floor were as colourful as the bowls of fruit on the small wrought iron tables, while a chandelier of the same delicate filigree served as the main source of illumination. Flowering creepers flourished in the four corners and the green fingers trailing up the tinted walls gave the room a hot-house aspect, accentuated by the orchids and magnolias that filled the white marble fireplace.

Above the mantelpiece a portrait of an older man looked down on her, the tapering fingers curving on a cigarette in a gold holder. There was a strength of purpose in the face that matched the arrogance of his bearing and Amalia caught Lorna's questioning glance.

'That's Manoel's uncle, Rafael's father. He died two years ago.'

'He looks very forbidding. Is his son anything like him?'

'The image – in looks *and* character. They were both very proud and put family honour before anything.

When Rosalia ran away—' she stopped, 'but let's not gossip. Drink your tea, before it gets cold.'

Lorna's curiosity was stirred. 'Who's Rosalia?'

'Rafael's sister.— but we don't talk about her. It was stupid of me to mention her name.'

'Why? What did she do? You can't not tell me now you've begun.'

Amalia looked round carefully before she spoke. 'She eloped with an Australian.'

'How romantic!'

'My uncle didn't think so. She was already engaged to Juan Diniz and he was furious. Everything had been arranged – the dowry, a settlement of land and a wonderful house. You've no idea the scandal it caused. The Diniz family were even more proud than my uncle and they took the elopément as a personal affront to their son. Not that I blame Rosalia entirely. Juan was a bit of a stick and Frank was very good-looking.'

'What happened in the end?'

'Nothing. I think she wrote once or twice, but my uncle tore up the letters without reading them. Rafael would do exactly the same if he had the chance. He'll never forgive her or allow her to return.'

'How can he stop her coming back if she wants to?'

'Easily. He's the head of the household and his word is law.'

'What a pig-headed man he must be! I'd never allow a brother of mine to stop me from coming home.'

'You've never had a brother like Rafael. Wait until you meet him.'

'When will he be here?'

Amalia laughed. 'Not for a few hours yet – so you needn't worry! As a matter of fact he's in Africa. There was some mix up over a delivery of cork and he flew out to settle it.' She held up a dish of cakes. 'These are much better than the last lot I offered you. Try the one with the cherry on top.'

They settled down to reminisce about the past and it was not until a maid came in to clear the tea-things that Amalia became conscious of the time.

'Good gracious! I promised to take you up to Aunt Isabella.'

'Is she ill?'

'She's never been really well since my uncle died. She spends the day in her room and only comes down for dinner when Rafael is here. I don't think he likes it much, but Aunt refuses to listen to him. As they say in England, a chip off the old block – but you'll soon find out for yourself.'

The dowager Senhora Rodriguez was exactly as Lorna had imagined. Tiny, wizened, with heavily lidded eyes and a thin, straight mouth, she looked every inch a matriarch. Her accent was surprisingly good and only occasionally did she hesitate for a word.

'I hope you will be happy here, Miss Fairfax. You will find life very different from England. Do you live in the country when you are home?'

'Not now, but I used to.' Anticipating her hostess, Lorna briefly outlined her past, and the old lady relaxed and smiled.

'It is good that you are used to a quiet life, for ours is very simple. The modern generation cannot appreciate anything that is old and tranquil. Amalia's life in Rio de Janeiro was full of excitement and now she must learn to relax; I think you will be good for her.'

Lorna refrained from saying that her reasons for coming to Portugal had been exactly the opposite: the Senhora seemed a woman who would brook no opposition.

'Come to the balcony, Miss Fairfax, and see my view. I am very proud of it.'

She drew back the shutters and pointed out Estoril sprawling below them. In the gathering dusk it was a fairy-tale city; the promenade lights like a string of pearls dividing the inky blackness of the sea from the shadow of the land.

'It is beautiful, is it not? But then perhaps I am, as you say, prejudiced?'

'Has this always been your home?'

'Since my marriage. My own family come from the Algarve — one of the loveliest of our provinces. We must arrange to take you there. It is well worth seeing.'

'I don't want Lorna dashing all over the country without me,' Amalia pouted. 'Wait until I've had the baby.'

'When that time comes,' her aunt said, 'you will have to go back to Brazil. It is my son's wish.'

'I wouldn't dream of leaving you, Amalia,' Lorna put in hastily. 'After all, the only reason I came was to keep you company.'

There was a momentary silence and Senhora Rodriguez smiled.

'I can see you are a diplomat, Miss Fairfax. It is a good thing. You will need to be while you are here.'

CHAPTER TWO

LORNA settled down on the Quinta as though she had been there all her life. How easy it was to get used to luxury, to do nothing all day but lie in the sun or go down to the beach for a swim. Owing to some quirk of the Gulf Stream the waters along the coast were icy cold and her dream of lazing in a warm sea received a rude awakening.

'Whatever do they keep in the water – refrigerators?' she dashed up the beach and vigorously dried herself on a towel.

Amalia looked up from beneath a parasol. 'Cold water's healthy, so your countrymen say! Be a dear and get some drinks – that'll soon warm you up.'

Lorna slipped on a cotton coat and pattered up the steps to the promenade. A row of faces looked down on her and she bit her lip to stop herself from smiling. She would never forget the first day Luiz had driven them to the beach! The station that linked Estoril to Lisbon cut across the esplanade and one had to cross the railway line to reach the steep flight of steps that led down to the narrow promenade. It was here that male passengers passed their time when they were waiting for a train, and feminine sunbathers had to run the gauntlet of whistles and cat-calls before reaching the comparative safety of the beach café.

Today was no exception, and by the time Lorna returned with two fruit drinks she was flushed and panting.

'You'll go for the next lot, old girl. I've never seen such a pack of wolves!'

'Blame your figure. I'm quite jealous of it myself.' She sat up and sipped her iced lemon. 'I can't understand why you're not married yet, Lorna, you're so pretty when you let yourself go. You should always wear your hair loose. I can't bear it in that ugly bun. It makes you look like an old maid.'

Echoes of her aunt came into Lorna's mind and she smiled ruefully. 'You're the second person to tell me that. Perhaps I'll have it cut while I'm here.' She began to rub suntan lotion over her arms and legs. 'What a pity I didn't bring a two-piece costume – I could have tanned all over then.'

'Not unless you want to end up in prison! Two-pieces are illegal here, but it's part of the fun to defy the beach policeman. You should see the flurry when he's sighted!'

'I can just see that happening in Blackpool!' Lorna turned over on her back. 'Wake me up when it's time to go.'

'We can't leave too late. Inez Castro is coming to dinner.'

'Who's she? Another relation?'

'Not yet, but she's hoping to be. My uncle wanted Rafael to marry her.'

'I'm surprised he hasn't popped the question, then.' Lorna's voice was muffled in her arms. 'I thought he was such a loyal son!'

Amalia laughed. 'His loyalty hasn't stopped him wanting a fling first! When he does settle down, though, I daresay it'll be with Inez. They understand one another very well. I think you'll like her.'

Privately Lorna doubted it. She had formed her own opinion of Rafael's character, and that Inez liked him was no recommendation. Indeed she did not feel drawn to any of the Rodriguez family, and the more she saw of Manoel the less she approved his flattering remarks and attentive manners.

As Amalia had predicted, her aunt was in the drawing-room entertaining her guest when they arrived home, and Lorna thought her the loveliest creature she had seen. Spanish in appearance, she moved with a grace and languor belied by the alertness of large, amber-coloured eyes. Everything about her was simple and subtle; a perfectly plain black dress revealed flounces of hidden pleats as she crossed slim ankles, and dark, oiled hair was drawn back over pointed ears into an unexpected plait on the nape of her neck.

It was obvious during the evening that there was an understanding between the Senhora and her young guest, for Rafael's name kept recurring as if it were the bond that drew them together. Lorna's interest stirred. What sort of man could attract a woman like Inez? Whatever it was there were two things they had in common – arrogance and an implicit belief in themselves.

'Will you be staying here long?' Lorna started and looked into the direct, liquid glance.

'Until Amalia has had her baby.'

'In that case you'll have time to visit my father's ranch before you go back. He breeds the best bulls in Portugal, and it would be an interesting experience for you to see them being rounded up.'

'It's very kind of you,' Lorna murmured, 'but please don't bother.'

'It is no bother. We can make up a house-party and Rafael can escort you all.'

Lorna hid a smile. So that was the reason behind the invitation. The young master was more elusive than she had imagined.

The following morning Amalia awoke with a migraine and there was little Lorna could do to help. Having seen her settled she went to her room, collected her sketching things and wandered downstairs into the garden. A small Moorish pavilion stood near the terrace and she sat down on a marble seat in its shade and picked up her sketch book and crayons. It was difficult to catch the exotic beauty around her, but soon she was absorbed in her task, her sun-bleached head bent over the pad, her fingers moving carefully.

'I can see we will have to commission you as artist to the Rodriguez family. You have caught the line of the magnolias extremely well.'

With a start that sent the point of her crayon across the page Lorna looked up into dark, deep-set eyes. There was no need to question who it was – the resemblance to the portrait was remarkable – even to a cigarette held in a small gold holder.

'I'm sorry I startled you,' he apologized. 'Now I have spoilt your drawing.'

He took it from her and looked at it. 'It is very good. You should have lessons.'

'Thank you, I already have.'

'Ah, I have said the wrong thing. Forgive me.'

His English was almost faultless – slow and deliberate, with a habit of drawling any word unfamiliar to him.

'Perhaps we should introduce ourselves,' he continued. 'I am Rafael Francisco Oliveira y Rodriguez. You are Miss Lorna Fairfax, are you not?'

'I am. How do you do?'

They shook hands and he sat on the seat beside her, while out of the corner of her eye she took in his fastidious appearance. As if conscious of her scrutiny he glanced at her in amusement and she hastily turned away.

'You like it here, Miss Fairfax?'

'How could I do otherwise? Your home is beautiful, senhor.'

'The most beautiful in Portugal.' His finality closed the subject. 'I hope you are keeping my cousin happy? Unfortunately she finds her compatriots too restricted in outlook; no doubt the fault of her upbringing. I am against my countrywomen being educated abroad.'

'I think it's a wonderful idea to see other people, other customs,' she said warmly.

'But this is your first time abroad, is it not?'

She subsided. 'Yes.'

'Then you are hardly in a position to recommend it to

others.' Carefully he fitted a fresh cigarette into the holder. 'No. If Amalia had been educated here she would not have needed the services of an English companion to amuse her. As it is, she is bored by everything except the horse-racing in Rio de Janeiro which she learned to like in England!'

Lorna burst out laughing, and after a moment he consented to smile.

'You may find it amusing, Miss Fairfax, but it has its difficulties.' He looked at his watch and stood up. 'It is late and my mother is expecting me for coffee. I will see you again at dinner.'

Lorna picked up her crayon. What a rude, conceited man! In a few minutes of conversation he had criticized her drawing, laughed at her opinions and as good as told her she ought to practise what she preached. Well, one thing was certain – she would do her best to avoid his company.

This was easier said than done, for in the next few days she was continually meeting him about the house. How different the tempo was now that he had returned; the little maids flew around even more industriously, the Cadillac and black shiny Rolls were polished to a higher brilliance, and Luiz followed at his master's heels like a faithful spaniel. He had only to raise his voice or crook a little finger and there was someone waiting for his command. The only person who did not stand in awe of him was his mother, and he treated her with a gentle raillery he displayed to no one else. He was certainly no fool, and she had to admit he was right about Amalia, for as time went on she became more and more distraught at her husband's nightly disappearances to Lisbon or the Casino.

It was the final blow when Manoel telephoned to say he could not come home for her birthday dinner. Sick with disappointment, Amalia ran into Lorna's room and flung herself down on the bed.

'This is the last straw!' she cried. 'He's always making excuses to stay away. He's ashamed of me, that's what it is.' She went to the mirror and gazed at her swollen figure with distaste. 'Look at me – ugly and fat – I'm not a bit like the girl he married.'

'Of course not! And you should be proud of it, not ashamed! I've never heard anything so silly.'

'Manoel isn't proud of me,' Amalia said bitterly. 'I wish we'd never come back to Portugal – I hate it here! In Brazil the women don't have to stay at home and look after a house and children.'

'Neither do you,' Lorna retorted, 'so I don't know what you're complaining about.'

'That's just it. Even though I *have* no ties I can't go out with Manoel. Over here a married man of our class would lose face if he took his wife everywhere. It just isn't done.'

Lorna could not deny the truth of this. In the few short months of her sojourn in Portugal she had learned enough to know that Manoel's behaviour was the normal one, and the fact that Amalia's marriage would not have satisfied her did not give her the right to criticize.

'Perhaps it'll be better once you've had the baby,' she said soothingly.

Amalia shook her head. 'All Manoel's friends are married, yet they're hardly ever at home. No matter what sort of life a girl leads when she's single, the minute she's married she might as well enter a convent.'

'But that's ridiculous! Why do they put up with it?'

'Why do women agree to harems? Because they don't know better.' She laughed mirthlessly. 'I'm emancipated, but what good has it done me?'

'Never mind, you'll soon be returning to Brazil.'

'That's the trouble; I don't think we are. Manoel said Rafael might want us to stay here.'

'Why don't you tell him you don't want to?'

'I daren't. Rafael's word is law and he never listens to me about business.'

'How would it be if I spoke to Manoel?' The minute the words were out Lorna was sorry. Her position was difficult enough without interfering between husband and wife. But there was no drawing back now. Amalia's face had brightened at the suggestion and she caught hold of Lorna's arm.

'If only you could make him see that we'd be much happier in Brazil! Oh, Lorna, I'm sure he'd listen to you! You and Rafael are the only two people he takes any notice of.'

Lorna sniffed. 'Senhor Rodriguez takes too much on himself. Why, even if Manoel wanted to spend an evening with you his cousin would probably tell him his behaviour wasn't in keeping with his social position!'

Her voice rang out sarcastically and Amalia was unable to hold back a smile. 'You'd better be careful, Lorna. You'll put Manoel's back up criticizing Rafael.'

'Then I'd better say nothing at all, because I certainly couldn't say what I had to without bringing him into it. I've never met such an interfering, autocratic man. But no more talk now. Wash your face and come downstairs for dinner and afterwards we'll have a nice quiet game of Canasta!'

But waiting in the drawing-room Lorna's qualms returned. No matter how much she tried she could not alter the customs and traditions of a country, and to interfere between husband and wife could only make matters worse. Would she never learn to curb her impetuosity?

She was startled by a knock on the door and looked up to see a maid beckoning her across the hall towards the library.

It was the first time Lorna had entered the room and she could not help appreciating its wonderful proportions. The high ceiling and large french windows were open to the night – the walls were lined with hand-tooled books. An ornate, carved desk stood in front of a marble fireplace, a brass reading lamp on its top throwing a circle of light on the red Turkey carpet. It was here that Rafael Rodriguez waited, his face cold and set.

'Good evening, Miss Fairfax. I would like to talk to you. Please sit down.'

Lorna did so, and he looked at her for a long moment before he resumed : 'I have just overheard a most illuminating conversation between you and my cousin. I credited you with more sense, but evidently I was wrong.'

Her face flushed. 'You weren't meant to hear!'

'Obviously. But Amalia left your door open and you have a particularly penetrating voice. I heard enough to convince me that you can do my cousin untold harm.'

'How dare you!' Anger overcame discretion. 'It's you and your ridiculous customs that—'

'Hardly my custom,' he rapped out. 'You are forgetting yourself, Miss Fairfax. Amalia knew exactly what she was letting herself in for when she married Manoel. He is no better or worse than anyone else, and she must accept it.'

'She never will.'

'Then no one can help her.' He paused as if to control himself and when he continued his voice was low and more gentle. 'Believe me, Miss Fairfax, I know what I am saying. I should be extremely reluctant to ask you to leave, but I cannot have you interfering in affairs that do not concern you and which you do not understand.'

'I understand very well,' she retorted. 'And I think it ridiculous for a woman to retire into the background the minute she marries.'

'Ridiculous or not, you cannot fight the traditions of a country. This "background" you refer to so scathingly is not a condemned cell. Amalia can find plenty to amuse her if she wants to.'

'Gossiping and hen parties!'

'Precisely. But women usually find it enough!'

'Not in England, senhor. This is the twentieth century — not the Victoria era!'

'Women were as happy then as they are today,' he countered, 'possibly happier.'

'I doubt it. Nowadays husbands and wives are on equal terms. We wouldn't call a marriage a happy one where the husband goes one way and the wife another.'

'The husband might go his way, Miss Fairfax, but the wife certainly does not go hers. She remains in her proper place — the home.'

'Then you should look for a slave when you marry — not a woman.'

His eyebrows lifted. 'I was not aware that I was under discussion.'

He stood up and came so close that she could smell the faint perfume of shaving lotion and hair cream. 'I have been speaking to you as the head of a Portuguese household,' he said quietly, 'not as a man. My own ideas of marriage happen to be different, but I am not prepared to discuss them with you now.'

'Meaning that *you* don't practise what you preach either?' She was glad to be able to hit back at him. 'You once said the same thing to me, senhor.'

'So I did.' He flicked an imaginary speck of dust from his sleeve. 'But come, you are hedging. Have I your promise to say nothing more to upset Amalia?'

'I never have upset her,' Lorna said angrily. 'Can't you understand that? We think alike because we had the same upbringing, but she might have had exactly the same ideas if she'd been brought up here. What about your sister? Living in Portugal all her life didn't stop *her* from breaking away.' Abruptly she stopped. 'I'm sorry, that was a dreadful thing to say.'

'It was.' His face was tired and drained of colour. 'I think you've said enough for one evening. You'd better go before I lose my temper.'

Cowed, trembling, and fighting back the desire to cry, she ran from the room.

When she entered the dining-room later that evening Amalia was already seated, her face as pale as the magnolias that patterned the centre of the table. The candles in the gleaming candelabra threw grotesque shadows on the ceiling and Lorna was glad that the semi-darkness hid her burning cheeks. She was still smarting from her interview in the library, and would have given anything never to see the house or its owner again. But she was not a free agent. She had come to stay with Amalia and one look at her friend's dejected face told her it would be impossible to walk out now. Much as she disliked doing so the only alternative was to apologize to Rafael.

'You're very quiet, Lorna,' Amalia came out of her reverie sufficiently to notice her friend's preoccupation. 'Is anything wrong?'

'Just a slight headache – I think it's the sun.'

They continued to eat in silence and as soon as the meal was over took their coffee cups out on the terrace. Reflectively Lorna gazed into the darkness at the fireflies darting among the long grass, her eye suddenly caught by a glow of light at the bottom of the steps. It remained stationary, wavered, then came nearer, and with a start she realized it was the glowing end of a cigarette. Slowly Rafael came up the steps and punctiliously inclined his head.

'Is it not a little damp for you to be sitting here without a wrap, Amalia?'

His cousin stood up instantly. 'I'd just finished my coffee and was going in – I'll see you in the morning Lorna.'

Lorna scrambled out of the hammock. 'Wait for me – I'm coming too.'

'There's no need for both of you to desert me. It is a beautiful evening, Miss Fairfax. Stay until I've finished my cigarette.'

Lorna sat on the edge of a chair, one slim leg tapping nervously on the floor. Rafael smoked in complete silence until with an expert flick of his finger the glowing butt rose in an arc and disappeared among the bushes. Immediately she stood up.

'Where are you going?'

'To my room. You've finished your cigarette.'

He smiled grimly. 'You needn't take me quite so literally – that was merely an excuse to talk to you.'

Lorna seized the opportunity. 'I'm surprised you still want to after the rude way I behaved. I'd like to apologize. Not for what I said about Amalia – I still think I'm right there – but because I had no right to bring your sister into it.'

'Thank you,' his voice was grave. 'I know how hard it is for you to apologize. And now I suggest we forget it and begin again. We have already wasted too much time. Sit down, Miss Fairfax, I won't bite!' He lit another cigarette. 'How are you getting on with your drawing? Have you done any more?'

'Not since that day in the pavilion.'

'A pity. I thought my praise might have encouraged you.'

'Hardly praise. If I remember rightly you advised me to have some lessons!'

'Because I am a perfectionist.'

'Nothing is perfect.'

'I don't agree. You can get a perfect flower or jewel or painting – even a perfect woman, if you're lucky.'

'I doubt it,' she said dryly. 'I don't think there is such a person. You might be able to find an ideal *hausfrau,* if that's what you want.'

'Not at all. I like someone with spirit. That's why I admire English and American women; they are used to standing on their own feet.'

'Quite often it's a case of having to.'

'Agreed, but they enjoy it none the less. Don't you?'

'Whether I do or not makes no difference. I have no choice.' In spite of herself a note of sadness crept in and he was quick to detect it.

'You are alone in the world?'

'No, I live with my aunt. But my parents died a few years ago and we had to give up our home.'

'That is always regrettable. I would never give up mine.'

'I'm sure you'll never have to,' she said politely, and thought of the estates in Brazil and East Africa, his magnificent house and all the luxury that went with it. She rose to her feet.

'Now, I really think I'd better go to bed. It's getting late.'

He stood up with her. 'We must show you something of our country while you are here. There is a market at Cascais which is well worth seeing.'

'The fish market?'

'No, there's a much larger one held each month — usually on the twenty-third.'

'Tomorrow, you mean?' The words were out before she could stop them and she bit her lip in annoyance. 'Goodnight, Senhor Rodriguez,' she said hastily.

She was at the foot of the stairs when he called after her, a hint of laughter in his voice, 'By the way, I *did* mean tomorrow, Miss Fairfax. I will meet you in the hall at ten.'

Eating her crisp rolls and fresh farm butter in the dining-room next morning, Lorna wondered if in the cold clear light of day Rafael would regret his impulsive invitation.

'You are down early, Miss Fairfax.'

With a start that spilled her coffee on her dress Lorna looked up to see Rafael standing in the doorway.

'I am always down by eight-thirty.' Ineffectually she dabbed at her dress.

'Here, use my handkerchief.' He proffered a crisp white one, but she shook her head.

'No, I'll stain it. I'll have to manage.'

'I am sorry. It was my fault for coming in so quietly.' He leant against the arm of a chair. 'I have been told I have a habit of sneaking up on people, but in your case it was quite unpremeditated.'

'Meaning that you sneak up on others?'

'Occasionally!' His teeth flashed in a smile. 'You would be surprised at some of the interesting things I see! But we are wasting time. Run up and change and I'll wait for you in the hall. It's a pity to miss the bustle of the market.'

Within minutes Lorna was ready and preceded her host down the steps to an open roadster.

'What a lovely car,' she commented.

'It's too fast for Portugal,' he said as he slipped into the driving seat. 'The roads are too tortuous for speed. I use it when I travel to Spain or France.'

She looked at him curiously. 'You are the first big business man I've met! What does it feel like to be so important?'

'You cannot draw me on that question, Miss Fairfax. I might give the sort of answer you would hold against me one day.' He leant forward, switched on the radio and gay music filled the air. He hummed an accompaniment in a deep baritone and after a moment she joined in, catching the tune with ease.

'What is it?' she asked at the end.

'A *fado*. A sort of folk-song with a story. They are handed down from generation to generation and quite often get heavily embroidered on the way. But why have you stopped singing? This is the first time I've seen you looking pleased with life.'

By this time they were driving along the coast road and

with a wave of his hand Rafael pointed out the home of two ex-kings. Within minutes the little square of Cascais was in sight and Lorna stared at the animated scene in front of her as the car drew to a standstill. Never had Lorna seen so much colour or confusion, and laughing, they got out of the car and pushed their way through the crowds, Rafael's hand hard on her arm.

Everything a countryman could want was on sale. Baskets, rag-rugs, blankets made from local wool, beans, rice, oil and the most delightful glazed pottery in brilliant yellow, blue or green.

'I must get some of those for my aunt,' Lorna said eagerly. 'Are they expensive?'

'A few escudos. An old man I know has a stall higher up. We can go to him.'

'Do you know everybody here?'

He grinned. 'No, but this fellow worked for us until his son gave him a stall to look after. I honestly think he was happier on the land.'

'Why doesn't he come back to you, then?'

'He's too proud. We Portuguese are.'

He guided her to a stall at the edge of the square, and as they approached, an old man hurried forward and caught Rafael's hand, tears streaming down his cheeks. Embarrassed, Lorna turned away and began to examine the pottery, picking out three bowls in different colours. To her disgust Rafael refused to let her pay.

'I wouldn't have mentioned them at all if I'd known,' she said indignantly.

'Nonsense.' He placed the package in her hand and bent his head so that their eyes were almost on a level. 'You should learn to accept a present more gracefully, Miss Fairfax. It doesn't become you to argue.'

It was late when they returned home, lunch had long been finished and Amalia had left a message that she had gone to her room for a rest.

'Oh, dear, I hope she isn't annoyed that I was away so long.'

'You are a companion, not a slave!' Rafael came back across the hall. 'I've asked them to lay the table on the terrace. It is cooler to eat there.'

'Are you staying for lunch?'

'I have kept the whole day free.'

Unaccountably Lorna was pleased, and during their meal found herself answering his questions about her life with a candour and frankness equalling his own. He listened sympathetically as she told him of her desire to escape from the routine of a commercial office and the closed circle of a surburban life.

'Not that there's anything wrong with a man who catches the five to nine every morning,' she added. 'But I wanted to see a bit more of the world and meet different people before I settle down.'

He glanced at her hand. 'You are engaged?'

'Oh no. At least, I could be, but I can't make up my mind.'

'Then you are not in love. If you were there would be no hesitation. You remind me of the princess in the fairy story waiting for the kiss that will wake her from sleep.'

'I've waited a long time, then,' Lorna said with a smile.

'I am glad.'

His voice was low and though he did not come near her it was as if she were imprisoned in his arms. She was stifled by a desire to escape, a longing to run away and remain inviolate.

'Hullo, you two. I hope I'm not interrupting.' Poised and beautiful, Inez sauntered out on the terrace and with a sigh of relief Lorna sank back in her chair. The Portuguese girl spoke to Rafael in an undertone and he raised his eyebrows slightly, replying in a flood of language that Lorna found unintelligible.

Inez shrugged and turned away. 'I'm sure Miss Fairfax would have understood if you had explained that you

T—B

were in a hurry.' She looked directly at Lorna. 'Rafael is such an excellent guide he couldn't bear to lose an opportunity of airing his knowledge. But my father is opening the International Jewel Fair in Lisbon and we have promised to be there.'

'I'm sorry,' Lorna murmured. 'I didn't know.'

'It is not important, merely irritating.' Inez smiled up at the man. 'If we had thought of it earlier, darling, we could have taken Miss Fairfax with us.'

'It is still not too late.'

'Please don't bother about me,' Lorna said quickly. 'I'm perfectly all right on my own.'

'Then everybody is happy,' Inez said tartly, and slipped her arm through Rafael's.

Together they walked along the terrace and Lorna watched them disappear, wishing crossly that they had not used her as a bone of contention. Her position was difficult enough without Inez making it worse. Yet the Portuguese girl's arrival had broken up a dangerous moment, a moment when she had almost been swept away by the proximity of a virile, powerful man.

The afternoon stretched ahead with no one to talk to, and after a moment's hesitation she hunted out her drawing pad and made her way down to the pavilion. She was half way up the shallow steps before she realized Rafael's mother was inside.

'I'm sorry, senhora,' she apologized, 'I'd no idea you were there.'

'That is quite all right, you are not disturbing me.' The greying head nodded to a wicker chair within the portico and Lorna sat down. It was cool inside the pavilion, the depth of green that surrounded it excluding the fierce rays of the sun.

'I hear you went to the market this morning. Did you enjoy it?'

'Very much.'

'Good.' The woman shifted her position so that she

could look at Lorna more closely. 'I get little chance to talk to you on your own. How are you settling down here — are you happy with us?'

'Of course.'

'But eager to get back, I suppose. Perhaps you have a young man in England? Over here no woman would rest if she were as old as you and still single.'

Lorna strove to hide a smile. 'In England I'm considered quite young. How old was your daughter when she married?'

'My daughter? Who told you about my daughter?'

For the second time Lorna wished the ground would open and swallow her. 'Forgive me,' she stammered, 'I shouldn't have mentioned it.'

'No matter, no matter,' the old lady said sharply. 'It is no secret that I had two children. But I am not used to people talking about Rosalia — since she ran away we do not mention her name.'

'Why?' Lorna said impetuously. 'There's nothing so terrible in what she did. Lots of girls elope.'

'In England perhaps. But over here we have our own traditions and beliefs, and as long as you stay with us you must respect them.'

'I do, I do! But it is difficult to respect something you don't understand.' She flung out her hands. 'I can't really believe you've cut your daughter out of your life. That you don't want to know if she's happy and well.'

'You have *got* to believe it!' The answer was sharp, staccato. 'I never want to see her again. She must never come back — never! Rafael would kill her!'

'Because she chose to live her own life?' There was no answer. Lorna shook her head. 'The whole thing seems too mysterious. I can't understand it.'

'There is no mystery,' the old lady said loudly, 'no mystery at all.' The blue-veined hands clenched on the arms of her chair and then relaxed as she sank back.

'Now if you will excuse me – I am tired. I would like to rest a little.'

Walking upstairs to see Amalia, Lorna pondered the feelings of a mother who refused to see her daughter merely because she had eloped, trying to excuse the Senhora on the grounds of hurt pride.

Amalia was lying on the bed reading a magazine when Lorna entered her room.

'You were late getting back,' she accused. 'I waited lunch until the omelette was flat. Where's Rafael? I thought he might have kept you out all the afternoon.'

'He's gone with Miss Castro to the opening of a Jewel Fair.'

'Of course, I was forgetting it began to-day. All the leading Portuguese families are displaying their heirlooms and the Rodriguez pearls will be on show.' She walked heavily over to the dressing-table and returned with a pearl and diamond brooch. 'Manoel gave me this when we were married.'

Lorna exclaimed at the intricate setting and workmanship, and Amalia nodded casually.

'This is nothing, Manoel's only a cousin of the family. You should see what Rafael's bride will get. I must ask him to show you one day.'

'No, thanks.'

'Why not? He's very proud of them. Some of the pearls are as large as halfpennies and there are two pear-shaped drops that are priceless.'

'Does he only collect pearls?'

'Mainly. Each family collects one kind of jewel; it's a sort of convention over here. Inez's family are renowned for their emeralds – but then theirs are nothing compared to the Diniz collection.'

Lorna pricked up her ears. 'Where have I heard that name before?'

'From me, probably. Juan Diniz – the son – was engaged to Rosalia and her ring was the largest emerald I've ever seen. The stone was almost as long as your finger with two rose-coloured diamonds either side. I believe she was afraid to wear it.'

'I'm not surprised,' Lorna said dryly. 'I would be too.' She hesitated. 'Don't think I'm prying, but earlier this afternoon your aunt said something about Rosalia that puzzled me. Why is everyone so bitter about her? Surely it's not only because she ran away?'

This time it was Amalia who hesitated. 'No,' she said slowly, 'it was much worse than that. She took the emerald with her.'

'What? You mean she . . .

'Exactly what I said. Now you can understand why we hate to talk about her. The fact that she eloped was bad enough, but the ring was priceless – part of a set that belonged to Queen Maria the First.'

'Couldn't they get it back?'

'Do you think Rafael didn't try? He flew to Australia, but Frank – that's her husband – refused to let him see her. He said she was ill in hospital and that any arguments might prove fatal. Anyway, I don't think Rafael could have done anything. The emerald was so large it could have been broken up into small stones or else bought as it was by a collector.'

'What happened in the end?'

'My uncle disinherited Rosalia and died soon afterwards. Everything was left to Rafael – the estates, the factory and this house.'

'Surely they would have been his automatically?'

'No. Rosalia was my uncle's favourite and he always promised to leave her the house. I believe he wanted Rafael to settle in Brazil or East Africa, but when he died Rafael took over the business. He has never discussed Rosalia since.'

Lorna shuddered at the tragedy that had overtaken this proud family. Terrible for someone of Rafael's heritage and pride to have to admit that his sister was a thief.

If she were Rosalia she would not rest knowing there was a man in this world who hated her so much.

'Don't tell anyone I told you the story,' Amalia said fearfully. 'Rafael would be furious if he knew. He can't bear to be reminded of her.'

'I can understand why,' Lorna said carefully. 'I would not like to make an enemy of him.'

And to herself she added : nor even too close a friend.

CHAPTER THREE

Now that she had learned the truth about Rosalia, Lorna could believe the Senhora's assertion that Rafael would kill his sister if he saw her. Perhaps it was this that made his presence in a room overpowering, made her long to escape the dark eyes that always seemed to be watching her. She had only to hear his precise, even tones for her body to tremble; yet his anger was for Rosalia and there was no reason for her own absurd fear.

It was with a definite sense of relief that she learned that they had all been invited to the Castro ranch. A change of atmosphere would do her good; she was getting too fanciful and nervous. Never had any man impinged on her consciousness like this one, and in other surroundings, with other people, his dominating personality might lose its compelling force.

But no matter how much she tried to put him out of her mind she could not forget his criticism of her clothes and reviewed her wardrobe with the growing conviction that he had been right. There and then she decided to take his advice. She was tired of making ends meet and worrying about the future. Tomorrow could take care of itself — she was young and she wanted to look her best now.

Amalia was delighted with her decision. 'I wish I could come with you,' she sighed, 'but it's too hot and —'

'I wouldn't dream of it. I'll be able to manage perfectly well on my own. What I can't explain with my tongue I'll explain with my hands!'

'I'd love to see you! Shall I ask Luiz to drive you in?'

'No, thanks. I'd like to try your electric trains.'

'Once will be enough,' Amalia grimaced. 'The seats

were designed for well-upholstered women, not someone like you!'

Sitting on the hard wooden seat of the third-class compartment, Lorna remembered her friend's words and wished she had accepted her offer. But the journey was a short one and in a little over half an hour she was standing in the great Square of Dom Pedro, enchanted by the rows of seventeenth-century houses that divided the business from the residential part of the town.

The stately Avenida da Liberdade with its widely spreading plane trees was the main Avenue of the city, and she walked along its pavements, averting her eyes from the bold, curious stares of the men sipping their drinks at the café tables.

At the end of the Avenue was the steep Rua Augusta. Here was a veritable Aladdin's Cave, each window vying with its neighbour for style and colour. Standing on the narrow pavement, jostled by shoppers all speaking a language she could not understand, Lorna's confidence ebbed and nervously she entered a shoe shop that bore the comforting sign 'English Spoken'.

However, by midday she had completed her purchases, spending the hour before siesta in the cool gilt salon of a hairdresser.

Senhor Pedro exclaimed in delight as he unwound the heavy silver coil of hair. 'It is a pity to cut it,' he said in perfect English. 'Perhaps you can wear it braided round your head – typical English fashion, no?'

'No,' Lorna said firmly. She had certainly not come to Portugal in order to remain typically English. 'It's too hot for me to wear it like this,' she explained. 'I want it very short.'

'That would be sacrilege, senhorita! Allow me to evolve a special chignon —'

'No,' Lorna reiterated. 'I want it short. It's too heavy as it is.'

Reluctantly the man took out his scissors. 'If the fair

senhorita will allow me the pleasure of creating a style for her, I am sure there will be no need to cut it all off in order to make it comfortable.'

In the face of such optimism she did not have the heart to refuse. 'Very well, but you must cut it a little.'

Bending over the pink basin a few moments later she found it difficult to believe that she had finally encountered a hairdresser who was reluctant to cut hair. Usually they were only too eager to set to work with the scissors! Closing her eyes, she gave herself up to the delight of having her head massaged and washed in a heavily scented shampoo and sitting under the hum of a chromium drier.

Surveying herself some time later, she was amazed at the transformation that Senhor Pedro had evoked. Free of its confining pins, her hair fell loose to her shoulders, the ends curling softly under. As she moved her head each springing wave caught the light and glinted with a silver sheen. It framed her face, softened the contours of brow and cheek and gave her the same clarity of line, the same gentle, diffused colouring as a Botticelli Venus.

'Is the senhorita satisfied?'

'Very much so. You are an artist, senhor.'

The dark liquid eyes glowed. 'It is very rarely that an artist has such an exquisite model.'

With a mutual exchange of compliments Lorna paid the moderate bill and wended her way to the station, pausing frequently to glance at her reflection in the shop windows.

With Latin extravagance the Rodriguez family complimented her on the result of her excursion.

'You look years younger!' Amalia said candidly.

'That's a backhanded compliment if ever there was one!'

'Trust my wife to put her feet in it,' Manoel interposed.

'Foot, darling,' Amalia corrected. 'Not feet.'

'No matter. Lorna understands me. But it is truly

amazing, this difference in your appearance. Is it not so, Rafael?'

Throughout the discussion Lorna had been conscious of her host standing aloof at one side of the drawing-room. He had allowed no vestige of surprise to cross his face when she had come into the room earlier that evening and now, forced into the conversation, he murmured a polite acquiescence before turning back to survey the scene through the window.

'Insufferable bore!' Lorna thought, trying to hide her chagrin. 'As if I care what he thinks!'

It was a great disappointment when the day before their departure for the Castro ranch Amalia caught a chill and was confined to her room. Lorna offered to stay with her, but no one would hear of it except the Senhora.

'I agree with Miss Fairfax,' she said firmly. 'She came here as companion to Amalia and it is her duty to stay with her when she is ill.'

'Amalia is not ill,' her son contradicted, 'and Miss Fairfax is not a paid duenna. If I have my facts correctly she is here as Amalia's friend and should be treated as such.'

The old lady stiffened and there was a hint of annoyance in her voice. 'I think you should leave the decision to the person concerned.'

'There is no decision. I've already accepted Senhor Castro's invitation, and Amalia's ill health only excuses herself and Manoel.'

The younger man looked up at this, opened his mouth as if to say something and then thought better of it.

'Then there is nothing more to be said,' the Senhora concluded.

'Except that you might have consulted me,' Lorna's voice rang out, and there was a startled silence. Never had anyone questioned Rafael's authority so openly and he looked as if he found the experience amusing.

'Forgive me for not discussing it with you, senhorita. I took it for granted you wanted to go.'

'I do, but —'

'Well, you are going – so the matter is closed.' He stood up and put his coffee cup down on a table. 'What about a stroll in the garden? It is a long time since we admired the moon together.'

Conscious of his mother's disapproval and Manoel's sardonic glance, Lorna preceded him on to the terrace. They walked the length of the first lawn and came to rest by the edge of the lily pond, the reflection of the moonlight rippling its surface.

In the cool night air Lorna's anger evaporated. 'I always seem to disagree with you, senhor,' she apologized.

'It is the prerogative of a pretty woman to be contrary.'

'I didn't know you thought that,' she flashed back.

'Thought what? That you were pretty or that you were contrary?' He put his head on one side and surveyed her. 'As a matter of fact you're both – to a maddening degree.'

Lorna felt a warmth stain her cheeks and was glad that the moon was obscured by a thin film of cloud. But as always he sensed her emotions.

'There's no need to be embarrassed, Miss Fairfax. You should take compliments in your stride. Or are you, like most of your countrywomen, unused to receiving them?'

'Possibly, senhor. Englishmen are not fulsome in their praise. Besides, I didn't think you noticed.'

'Noticed what?'

'The way I look. Why, you never even —' she hesitated. 'I think it a little cold. Shall we go in?'

'It isn't in the least cold, and don't try and change the subject. If you were going to say that I didn't notice your new hairstyle, you're wrong. There's very little about you I am not aware of.'

'Then why didn't you comment on it? I've never known you at a loss for words when it comes to women, senhor.'

'Sometimes, Miss Fairfax, there is no need for words.

Besides, we Portuguese believe that eyes can be as eloquent as lips.'

'Then I'd better not argue with you any more. You're too quick for me.'

'On the contrary, I like a woman with spirit.' He dipped his hand in the pool and let the water trickle through his fingers. 'Why were you surprised when I told Manoel to stop here?' he asked suddenly.

Nonplussed at the accuracy of his perception, she blurted out the truth. 'I thought you believed a man should be free whether he's married or not.'

For a moment he was silent, then he sighed. 'You have odd ideas about me, Miss Fairfax. I sometimes think you want to believe the worst.'

'Not at all, senhor, but—'

'But – but – always buts! Can't you ever agree with what I say? It makes me nervous to know you are always waiting to pounce on me.'

'I can't imagine you being nervous of anything. You are a man of steel.'

'How little you know me! I must try and alter your opinion before I leave.'

'Are you going away?'

'Yes, I must keep an eye on the estate in Brazil. Money brings its responsibilities, you know – in this modern age one cannot be idle and rich!'

'Will you be there long?'

'Perhaps six months – maybe a little more.'

'In that case I shan't be here when you return. I'm only staying until Amalia leaves Portugal.'

'That may not be for some time. I am hoping to get married, and Manoel might have to take over some of my work here.'

Her hands grew suddenly moist. 'I'm surprised you have not married before, senhor.'

'The wish was there,' he said coolly, 'but the woman was not.'

Without knowing why, she lashed out at him, 'I can imagine you choosing a wife as deliberately and coldly as you do everything else.'

'Deliberately maybe, coldly – never.'

'And if the woman you choose does not want to marry you?'

'Women do not always know what is good for them,' he said with maddening deliberation. 'I hope this one will.'

'You have a very poor opinion of my sex, senhor, and a very high one of yourself.'

'Thank you. I believe it is justified.'

'By Portuguese standards, maybe,' she flashed, 'but not by mine.'

A red tide of colour rushed into his face and he caught her roughly by the shoulders. 'One day you will try me too far, senhorita! No one has talked to me like that and got away with it. You need to be tamed into submission and there are two ways of doing it. Beating' – his face came down to hers, 'or kissing.'

For what seemed an eternity his mouth was poised above her own, his breath warm on her cheek. Then with a little cry she wrenched herself free.

'Fortunately, senhor, I am not yours to tame. Good night.'

In the bustle of departure next morning there was no time for embarrassment. The Senhora was ensconced on cushions in the back of the car and Lorna had no choice but to sit beside Rafael in the front. His manner was as correct as always and it was difficult to reconcile his aloofness with the violence of the night before.

The drive ahead of them was a long one, for the Quinta or estate of the Castro family was in the province of Algrave in the southernmost part of Portugal. From Lisbon, they crossed the River Tagus by motor launch that threaded its way carefully beside the big ships and the little canoes that darted out of their way like 'water boatmen' on a pond.

It was mid-morning when they motored through Seturbal, and Lorna was intrigued by the pyramids of salt drying on the banks of the River Sado. But gradually cultivation became scarcer and expanses of rolling scrub land stretched out to horizons delineated by a line of jagged hills. There seemed to be no escape from the sun, and she was hot and grimy when Rafael drew the car in to the side of the road for lunch.

Resentfully she stared at the back of his smooth head as he lifted out the picnic basket. 'Don't you ever feel the heat, senhor? No one has a right to look as cool as you do.'

'I am used to it. In Brazil one has to change two or three times a day.'

'Is it because of the heat or the humidity?'

'Both. One can bear heat. It's the continual dampness that is trying. If you leave a pair of shoes in a cupboard for a week you're likely to find them covered in green mould when you take them out into the open.'

She shuddered. 'How horrible! I don't think I'd like to live there.'

'You can't say that without going. Brazil is a wonderful country and Rio de Janeiro the loveliest city in South America.'

The Senhora had decided not to have her lunch in the open air and in spite of her son's protests had insisted on remaining in the car. He bent to take out a flask of wine from the picnic hamper. Idly Lorna watched his strong, tanned hand manipulating the cork of the bottle.

'Ah.' He gave a satisfied sound as it came away in one piece. 'Pass me a glass and I'll pour you some.'

'I don't like to drink during the day. It makes me sleepy.'

'Nonsense.' He held the bottle aloft. 'You can't refuse a glass of our very best Portuguese wine! Of course,' he added modestly, 'it's not as good as the French...'.

She laughed. 'You're very persuasive, senhor. I'll have a little not to offend you.'

He filled a glass to the brim.

'I said a little,' she protested.

'I am not a man of half measures. One day you will know the truth of it.'

'Why do you always speak in riddles, senhor?'

'Eventually I will give you the answer to that too!'

Afraid to pursue the subject, she took the glass from him and placed it to her lips wrinkling her nose as the liquid coursed down her throat. 'It's a bit too sweet, I think.'

'Women usually like sweet wines.' His eyebrows raised. 'But I should have known that you would prefer something more dry.'

Her lips curved in a smile, but she refused to look at him and a few moments later they tidied the hamper and resumed their journey. In the car again it was difficult to resist the desire to sleep and gradually her eyes closed and she slipped down into the seat. She awoke to find her head on Rafael's shoulder and hastily drew away.

'I'm sorry, you should have pushed me off. Have I been asleep long?'

'Long enough to miss the most boring part of the journey.' He spoke quietly and glancing round she saw that his mother was dozing, her head buried in her chest. 'We are already in Algarve,' he continued, 'the loveliest part of my country.'

Lorna looked out of the window with interest. They were now running parallel with the sea and overtook several peasant women riding mules, dark kerchiefs over their heads and broad, black hats shading their faces. The white-washed houses were Moorish in design, with flat roofs and small windows, and the setting sun threw a path of gold across the surface of the sea.

'I could almost believe we were in Arabia.'

'You are observant,' he agreed. 'The Moors were in this part longer than in any other province, and a few of their customs still remain.' His eyes mocked her. 'Down here women are still regarded as chattels and their husbands' word is law!'

'A pity you don't live here, then, it would be very convenient for you.'

He laughed. 'You are never at a loss for words, are you, Lorna? You should have had red hair!'

'Perhaps I'll dye it for you.'

'Never!' he said emphatically. 'Being natural is part of your charm.'

'Thank you, senhor. That's the first *real* compliment you've paid me.'

'My name is Rafael. I would like you to use it.'

Her reply was forestalled as they turned sharply through heavy, wrought iron gates covered with wistaria and drove through a wild tract of land before entering an avenue bordered by well planned gardens. At once the house came into view; built in the shape of an L, its mediaeval appearance was heightened by a large number of windows and a stone archway above the door emblazoned with the Castro coat of arms.

Inez and her parents were at the step to greet them and Lorna was shown immediately to her room. As was usual in Portuguese houses the shutters were closed tight, and she pushed them open and leaned out, breathing in the warm, scented air. It was a matter of minutes to store her clothes away in the ebony wardrobe and by the time she was ready, the first dinner gong echoed from the hall.

There were at least twenty people at the long dining table, with Inez and Rafael side by side at the far end. Lorna was placed between two men who spoke neither English nor French, but she was too interested in her surroundings to mind.

The room was exceptionally lovely. Coloured tiles patterned the walls like paintings and the ceiling was covered with medallions illustrating the art of bull-fighting. Tall corner cupboards held priceless objets d'art and hand-woven curtains were drawn back to show a cloistered passage-way with a small fountain playing at the end of it.

It was only when they retired to the drawing-room and Inez still made no effort to draw her into the conversation that Lorna began to feel restless, bored, and then annoyed. Rafael, the centre of a group of men, did not look once in her direction, and she refused to acknowledge that she was hurt at his complete lack of interest.

She stood up to say good night and immediately he was at her side.

'Do you want anything?'

'No, thank you, I'm going to bed.'

'It's early yet.'

'I doubt if I'll be missed.'

'I'm sorry you feel lonely.' His mouth tightened as he looked at Inez in the far corner of the room.

'I'm not lonely,' she said quickly, 'but it was a long drive and I really am tired.'

He said no more as she bade good night to her host and hostess and was already engrossed in conversation when she went upstairs:

In her room Lorna pondered the strangeness of Inez's behaviour. The girl had not addressed one word to her the whole evening, and even when her parents had spoken in English she had quickly changed the conversation back into Portuguese. Yet they were a people who prided themselves on their hospitality, and Inez's rudeness was as unaccountable as it was strange. Unwittingly the word jealousy came into her mind, but she dismissed it as being absurd. What reason could this beautiful young aristo-crat have for being jealous of her?

Coming back from the bathroom she was startled to

see Rafael leaning against the doorpost of her room. Her heart jumped, but only by the widening of her eyes did she betray any surprise.

'I have been waiting for you, Lorna,' he said softly. 'I wanted to speak to you.'

'There was plenty of opportunity downstairs.'

He hesitated. 'The situation was a little difficult. It might have been embarrassing if I had singled you out.'

'I have no desire to be singled out,' she said coldly. 'I don't know why you should assume I have. Really, senhor, you can't ignore me the whole evening and then expect me to welcome you with open arms.'

'I don't think you'd welcome any man with open arms, Lorna, you are too cold. Sometimes I wonder whether you are capable of any passion and warmth at all.'

'There's no need to be insulting!'

'How typical of you to be insulted when I talk of passion! Have you no feelings, Lorna? I wish I knew what went on behind that beautiful face.'

Before she could move his arms were tight about her, his body straining close and his mouth, on hers, alive with desire. Instinctively her hands came up to the back of his neck, and at her touch his control snapped. Gone was the man who was master of his emotions – now they were mastering him, and Lorna was carried away on the flood of a passion that threatened to conquer her.

'Rafael, no! No!'

Instantly he released her. 'You are frightened, *pequeña*, I am sorry, I wouldn't hurt you for the world.'

Without a word she slipped past him into her room and turned the key in the door. There was nothing to say, no explanation to make. He had kissed her and she had responded to him. Better to leave it at that.

When Lorna went down for breakfast Inez was already seated at the table. The Portuguese girl looked pale and tired and greeted her with a conspicuous lack of warmth.

'I hope you slept well, Miss Fairfax.'

'Very well, thanks, but it's much warmer here than Estoril. I had to keep the windows wide open all night.'

'Because you're not used to the heat. There are a great many differences between your country and mine, senhorita, make no mistake about that. Climate is the most obvious one : temperament can too easily be over-looked.'

Instinctively Lorna felt she was being warned. But against what? Inez herself supplied the answer.

'Portuguese men are used to being the masters, and women like myself are brought up to believe that that is the way it should be.'

Lorna smiled politely. 'We have a proverb that says "An Englishman's home is his castle".'

'You might *say* that, but women of your sort don't believe it! No, I have been to England and seen your kind of marriages – cold, businesslike arrangements where the woman gives the orders.'

Lorna smiled. 'You're completely wrong, but I don't want to argue with you. What I would like to know is why you are telling me all this? I mean, you must have some reason.'

The amber eyes were veiled. 'Because I don't want you to get hurt. Rafael is attractive and very unscrupulous when it comes to "affaires de coeur"!'

Lorna's heart jumped. 'What has that to do with me?'

Inez shrugged. 'It is obvious you like him. I don't blame you, most women do. But he really shouldn't use our quarrels as a chance to flirt with every pretty girl that comes along. I keep telling him he will do it once too often, but he never believes me.'

Lorna forced herself to look into the beautiful, calm face. 'I think you are imagining things, Miss Castro. If I like Senhor Rodriguez it is because he is interesting and intelligent to talk to. I am surprised you should see more in it than that.'

'I did not want you to get hurt. That was all.'

'You have no need to worry about me. I am perfectly able to take care of myself.' Lorna bent her head to her breakfast. The sight of the food repelled her, but she forced herself to eat. Not for anything would she give Inez the satisfaction of knowing that her shafts had gone home.

'Good morning, Inez – Lorna.' Together with his host Rafael came into the room. 'You are both up early.' He turned to Lorna. 'Have you recovered from the journey?'

'It was hot for Miss Fairfax,' Inez interrupted. 'She could not sleep. I was just telling her it was a pity Amalia could not come. If I had known I would have invited a few more people who spoke English.'

'Never mind.' For the first time Senhor Castro spoke. 'It will give me a chance to practise mine!' He sat down and piled his plate with croissants. 'I thought we would all go up to see the bulls this morning. I am sure it is what Miss Fairfax has been looking forward to.'

'We are going riding this morning, Papa,' Inez said quickly. 'It will be too hot this afternoon. I am sure you can take Miss Fairfax on your own. Rafael won't want to see the bulls again.'

'Not at all,' Rafael said. 'I would like nothing better. We can all go and see the herd this afternoon.'

Left to her own devices, Lorna mused over the morning's conversation. Subtlety was not the Portuguese girl's strong point and she had made the position between herself and Rafael quite clear. Stupid to have believed that a man of his culture and wealth could be interested in someone like herself. It was as well Inez had explained the reason for his quixotic behaviour – to be forewarned was to be forearmed.

It was midday before the other women guests came downstairs, and Lorna found that her hostess and several of the other ladies present spoke English passably well once they had overcome their fear of not being understood.

As soon as lunch was over they piled into cars and drove the short distance to the bull ring, a large field enclosed by a high fence of sheet-iron. A low platform had been built alongside, and Lorna climbed on to it with others and looked down on a series of pens. Beside the last one stood a heavy horse-cart, and she looked at it curiously.

'The bull is driven into that when it's wanted for the arena.'

Rafael spoke into her ear, and Lorna drew back with a start, her reply drowned by pounding hooves as her host, mounted on a beautiful white stallion, rode into the enclosure, followed by twelve men on horseback. Each one wore the same livery of white shirt, red jerkin and leather shorts, in their hands long pikes with which to protect themselves.

'Those are the *campinos*. It is their job to attract the bulls.' Rafael indicated with his hand. 'Look over there and you can see them.'

She looked in the direction he was pointing and saw the herd standing quietly at the far end of the enclosure. Almost immediately the *campinos* fanned out and rode straight at them. The bulls tossed their heads, snorted angrily, and attacked.

At once the range was covered with charging animals and a cloud of dust rose into the air. Senhor Castro, erect on his white horse, sprang into the fray and the other riders galloped away leaving him to face the bulls. Half turning, he raced past the platform, the raging animals hard on his heels. Lorna's heart stood still as she saw that he was riding directly into another herd which had suddenly appeared in the distance. There could be no escape for him : without even a pike to protect him from the murderous horns he would be tossed to his death. But as he approached the new danger the bulls miraculously made a path for him and he rode straight through! With a gasp Lorna covered her mouth, and Rafael caught her arm.

'There's no danger,' he said soothingly. 'They are the bell cows and are used to entice the bulls into their pens. Look and you will see what I mean.'

As the two herds intermingled the bulls quietened down and, guided by the sharp pikes of the *campinos*, went docilely into their pens.

'The performance is now concluded.' The man looked at her white face and trembling lips. 'I think you have seen quite enough for one afternoon. I suggest something to bring you back to a more peaceful frame of mind.'

With an effort Lorna smiled. 'A hot cup of tea, I think!'

'A drive in the country would be a better suggestion. Excuse me.'

With a nod he walked to where Inez was standing with his mother. Although they were some distance away Lorna saw the young girl frown and make a gesture of protest, but Rafael turned on his heel and came back to her side.

'Ready?' he caught her elbow to guide her down the steps.

'Aren't the others coming?' she inquired.

'My mother is tired,' he said calmly, 'and Inez refused.'

Furious that she had not done the same, Lorna followed him to the car. If she changed her mind now he would want to know why : better to acquiesce and pretend it did not matter one way or the other.

She sat quietly by his side as they drove through some of the most wonderful country she had ever seen. In the hot, hazy sunshine every tree glittered as if it were alight; great heaps of grain and straw of palest gold lay drying on the earth, and the lumbering oxen, sweating in the sun, placidly pulled their carts along.

'It's all so beautiful,' she murmured.

'So were you last night. Like a golden candle – pure and cold – yet burning to the touch! I am sorry you ran into your room so quickly. There was no need to be afraid of me.'

'I am not afraid of you, senhor, but I have reached the age when I find flirtations rather dull.'

His mouth tightened. 'You never miss an opportunity to hurt, do you? One day I will remind you of all the unpleasant things you said to me.'

'I don't want to hurt you,' she protested, 'but I honestly don't know what to make of you.'

'Why make anything at all?' He glanced at her – a warm, vibrant look. 'Do not analyse and prove, *pequeña,* accept things as they come. It is much better so.'

There was nothing to say to this and she looked away. When he spoke to her so intimately she could almost believe Inez was lying. Yet the very fact that he was staying with the Castro family indicated that he had every intention of marrying the daughter.

They had tea in the garden of a red and white tiled pension, and Lorna saw another side of Rafael as he teased the fat, smiling patron into providing a tea more suitable for a banquet. Large, flat pancakes swimming in syrup and cream; crunchy rolls dipped in wild strawberry jam and then lightly toasted and an amazing assortment of small, rich pastries, the whole washed down by jasmine-scented tea.

Half way through, Lorna confessed herself full. 'You'll have to finish the rest. I couldn't manage another thing.'

'But I ordered it for you. I know English people like a – how do you call it – high tea?'

'Not quite as high as this!' she laughed. 'I'm not used to such rich food.'

He looked at her carefully. 'You could do with it, though. You have so much spirit and independence it is difficult to realize you are so fragile. I could break your wrist between my fingers.' He leaned forward and caught her hand. 'I wonder if you realize how tantalizing you can be. Fire and warmth one minute, icy disdain the next. A man might become annoyed with you, Lorna, but he would never become bored.'

'I can return the compliment.'

'The devil you can!' His lips curled in a half smile and he stroked her fingers. 'Lorna, Lorna, you have so little confidence in yourself and your beauty. That is what I like best about you. You are like a violet when I have always been used to orchids.'

She drew her hand away and busied herself with the teapot. 'New things have a novelty that is apt to wear off.'

'Possibly.' His face resumed its closed look and they finished their tea in silence.

It was late when they reached the Quinta and together they walked up the steps to the main salon. Manoel stood up at their entrance.

"What are you doing here? Rafael was the first to speak. 'When did you arrive?'

'Early this afternoon. Amalia was feeling better, so I decided to come along.'

"What a good idea! She can do with a change of atmosphere.' Lorna made for the door. 'I'll run up and see her. Which is her room?'

'Amalia's in Estoril,' Manoel said casually. 'I thought the drive would be too tiring for her.'

'Do you mean she's alone in the house?'

'The maids are there.'

'That beside the point. You're her husband and it's your duty —'

'Be quiet, Lorna!' Rafael's voice cut across hers. 'Do not talk to my cousin like that.'

The colour drained from Lorna's face and she drew back as if she had been slapped. Rafael took a step towards her, but she evaded his arm and without a word ran from the room.

To her disgust everyone accepted Manoel's appearance without his wife as if it were the normal code of behaviour, and Lorna knew that Inez had been speaking the truth when she said there was a difference in outlook between England and Portugal.

The evening dragged interminably. Twice Rafael tried to attract her attention, but resolutely she looked away. They had nothing to say to each other. Indeed, his rounding on her in defence of Manoel had hurt so much she was afraid to analyse why.

As soon as she could she excused herself on the pretext of a headache, and moving quickly about her bedroom began to pack.

She left early the following morning before anyone except the servants were afoot, and arrived at the shuttered house in Estoril as dusk was falling. Without pausing to take off her coat Lorna sped up the stairs to her friend's room.

Amalia greeted her with swollen eyes. 'Lorna darling, I didn't hear you come in! What's the matter? Where's the family?'

'Nothing's the matter, and the family are still in Algarve.' Puffing slightly, she sat down on the bed. 'I've had enough of Portuguese customs for one weekend!'

'How did you get here? Did anyone drive you?'

'Train, my love. And what a train! I could have walked more quickly! I don't think they've ever heard of restaurant cars and when I asked the ticket collector he thought I was mad. Still, I'm here, and that's the main thing.'

Amalia's eyes spilled with tears and she groped for her handkerchief. 'Oh, Lorna, you did it for me. You came because Manoel left me alone! You needn't deny it, because I know it's true.'

'Well, what if it is?' Resolutely Lorna kept her voice cheerful; it would not take very much for her to cry with

Amalia. 'I was looking for an excuse to get away, and you. were as good as any.'

'What did Rafael say when you told him? I bet he was furious.'

'He doesn't know — at least not until I'd already left.' She squared her shoulders. 'He might be the head of your family, my dear, but he's not the head of mine. I came here to be with you and no one is going to stop me.'

This last speech was too much for Amalia and she threw herself into Lorna's arms, sobbing as if her heart would break.

'Oh, Lorna, I don't know what I'd do without you! I never knew this house was so big or — lonely. I tried so hard to get better for Manoel, and the minute I said I felt fine he left me!'

'There's no point in talking about it now.' Lorna changed the subject. 'All this is between you and Manoel and I'd wait until you're feeling more like yourself before you have it out with him. Now come on. Put on your dressing-gown and come downstairs for dinner.'

Over a light meal Lorna recounted her weekend, and as she told the story of her afternoon's excursion with Rafael, Amalia's eyes glinted.

'Inez won't invite you there again if I know anything about her. The minute Rafael looks at another woman her claws come out. Not that she's had any reason to be jealous before,' she amended quickly. 'If Rafael's ever had any affairs he's always been most circumspect about them.'

'I'm sure someone so rich and popular must be greatly sought after.' Lorna's expression was ironic, but Amalia missed the sarcasm.

'He is,' she said seriously. 'And not only because he's rich, either. He's got a way of talking to you and looking at you as if you were the only woman in the world.'

Too well Lorna knew the truth of this. 'I still wouldn't envy his wife. When I marry I'd like to feel sure of my husband.'

'That's a matter of opinion. A husband you're too sure of can become boring, but then perhaps you're not looking for excitement in your married life!'

'At the moment I'd settle for contentment.' Unable to quell her curiosity, Lorna drew the conversation back to the person nearest her thoughts. 'But why doesn't he marry Inez? What's stopping him?'

'Your guess is as good as mine. If anyone's holding back it isn't her. I can't understand it. She's got everything he needs in a wife — breeding, background —' she hesitated, 'and nationality.'

'Do you think the same nationality is so necessary?'

'It helps. Marriage is difficult enough as it is.'

'An old-fashioned philosophy,' Lorna said quietly. 'A lot of people could prove you wrong. Wouldn't you have been happy married to an Englishman?'

'Yes, but then England was part of my life. For someone coming to a strange country it would be entirely different. Although Manoel and I quarrel we still share the same roots and believe in the same things. But why are we talking like this? I could no more imagine you marrying a foreigner than pigs flying! What about a game of Canasta? It will pass the time.'

'Right. Where are the cards?'

'In a green leather box in the corner desk, I think. If not they're in the library. I'll set up the card table in my bedroom and we can play there. Don't forget to bring a pencil and pad.'

But the desk in the corner of the drawing-room only held a stack of dominoes and a set of ivory carved chessmen, and Lorna had no choice but to go into the library. The very sight of the room reminded her of Rafael, and she moved to the desk, painfully aware of the personality of its owner. How she had hated him the first time she had seen him in this room. If only she could say the same thing now!

She opened the top drawer and stared down at the neatly clipped files. Nothing there. Nothing in any of the drawers except notepaper, clippings relating to the estate and small box files. In the bottom drawer she found what she was looking for — the pile of score cards and underneath the green leather box. Casually she flicked it open and an enormous emerald, flanked by two rose-pink diamonds, winked up at her! With shaking fingers she took it out and read the tiny letters inscribed on the platinum circlet — Juan Diniz.

This must be Rosalia's engagement ring — there could not be two emeralds like it in the world! But Rosalia had taken it away with her — or had she? Could it have been lying here unnoticed all this time? Impossible! If Rosalia had left it behind, it must have been discovered long ago, unless someone had deliberately hidden it in order to blacken her name. Yet who would have reason to do such a thing? Only one person had stood to gain — Rafael!

With a little cry she replaced the emerald in its box, slammed home the drawer and fled from the room. But nothing could shut out the dreadful suspicion that was forming in her mind.

CHAPTER FOUR

OBSESSED with her discovery of the ring, Lorna forced herself to behave to Amalia as if nothing had happened. But she was filled with hidden fears, and like the hydra-headed monster of mythology as she conquered one doubt another would grow in its place. Nowhere could she find relief from the irrefutable fact that Rafael had stolen the ring. Had he not told her himself that he would never give up his house? Yet he had known his father intended leaving it to Rosalia : what more natural than for him to succumb to the temptation of making her seem a thief? No matter which way she argued she could reach no solution. Everything was indicative of his guilt, and only her heart refused to believe he was the sort of man who would implicate the family honour to further his own ends.

What could she do? Tell the Senhora that her daughter was innocent and her son guilty or confront Rafael with the knowledge? Either course was anathema to her, yet to say nothing was even worse, and she was still torn with indecision when the family returned from Algarve.

She was walking with Amalia along the drive when the cream Cadillac swerved to a stop at the front door. Rafael helped his mother out and Lorna waited until he had turned to see the luggage before she came forward. Manoel greeted her easily, then placed an affectionate arm across his wife's shoulders as they disappeared into the house.

The old lady watched them go and shrugged. 'How easily young people forget their differences when they've been parted a few days.'

Leaning heavily on Lorna's arm, she mounted the steps and paused in the hall to gaze around.

'Ah, it is good to be home again. I always feel the pleasure of coming back far exceeds the pleasure of going.'

'Because your home is so lovely,' Lorna murmured.

'I am glad you think so, although that surely was not the reason you decided to leave the Castros so precipitately? They were most offended.'

'I'm sorry, Senhor. I left because of Amalia.'

'You should have told us.'

'I was afraid you'd try and stop me, and I felt it my duty to be with her.'

'And what about your duty as a guest?' Rafael had come up silently behind her. 'Your behaviour was insulting, to say the least.'

'I didn't mean it to be,' she said quietly. 'I've written and explained to Senhor Castro.'

'Of what use is a letter? Nothing can condone bad manners.'

'Or selfishness,' she flashed back. 'You once told me to mind my tongue, but you can't stop me thinking!'

'Obviously – even if what you think is wrong!'

'Children!' the Senhora admonished. 'Kindly do not shout, and if you must quarrel, please do so where the servants cannot hear.'

Rafael turned away disdainfully. 'I have no quarrel with Miss Fairfax. She behaves like a spoilt child and should learn some self-control.'

Lorna bit her lip; if only he knew how much control she was exerting! But she said nothing and helped the Senhora up the stairs to her room.

Lorna avoided Rafael's presence as much as posible for the rest of the week, delaying her appearance at the breakfast-table until he had left for Lisbon, and retiring early on the rare occasions when he was home for dinner. The very sight of his proud face and dark penetrating eyes unnerved her and she was afraid he would read her thoughts and question her.

It was not until the Sunday after their return from Algarve that she came face to face with him as she was crossing the drawing-room. Manoel and Amalia had gone for a drive and Lorna had decided to take her book into the garden. Now the man barred her way.

'Good afternoon, Lorna.'

'Good afternoon, senhor.'

'It used to be Rafael.'

She looked at a point beyond his shoulder. 'Rafael, if you prefer it. Now if you'll excuse me I'm going into the garden.'

'Why the hurry? It's much cooler here.'

'It's equally cool under the trees.'

'I'm sure it is if you say so, but for the moment I'd like you to stay with me.' His lips curved in a smile. 'Please sit down, Lorna, I want to talk to you.'

Reluctantly she obeyed and he moved back to the mantelpiece.

'I owe you an apology,' he began without preamble.

'For what?'

'Surely you know without my telling you.'

'I'm afraid I don't. I'm not a mind-reader.'

His eyes glinted. 'I see you're determined to get your pound of flesh! All right, you shall have it.' He put his foot on the fender. 'I apologize for being rude to you that afternoon at the Castros'. I knew the minute I had spoken that you resented it, but I was afraid your tongue would run away with you, and strictly speaking it was none of your business.'

'Of course it's my business!' Lorna burst out. 'Amalia's my friend.'

'That still does not give you the right to interfere between man and wife. Come, Lorna, you forget I am the head of the family and if any interfering must be done it is my place to do it.'

'But you condone his behaviour.'

'For the time being. If he goes too far —' his shoulders

lifted expressively, 'that is another matter. But we are
not discussing Manoel and Amalia now. At the moment
I am more interested in you.' his eyes darkened and
he moved a step towards her. 'Well, Lorna, what is your
answer? Will you forgive me?'

'Of course I forgive you, senhor. Such a beautifully
worded apology deserves nothing less.'

'Good. Then we are friends again.'

'I don't think we can ever be friends. Your ways and
mine are too different for that.'

'*Comos diabos!* Now what's the matter?' the breath
hissed sharply between his teeth. 'Ever since I returned
from Algarve you've been acting strangely. What's the
reason for it?'

'Nothing! Nothing!' She began to tremble, afraid of
his power over her, afraid too that she would blurt out
the truth. 'I – just don't like being spoken to as if I were
a servant. You – you treat women differently here – I'm
not used to it.'

'You're lying!' He caught her roughly by the shoulders.
'I demand the truth. Never have I apologized to a woman
before – never! Do you hear me? And I would not do so
now if it weren't because I wanted you, because I—'

'No, no!' Lorna broke in. 'Don't go on Rafael – I don't
want to hear!'

'But you shall,' he continued remorselessly. 'I'm tired of
all this petty behaviour. It is time we stopped —'

A discreet knock interrupted them and his hands
dropped to his side as a maid entered. Silently he listened
to the flood of Portuguese and when he turned round
again his face was set.

'Marie says a friend of yours is outside. A man called
Simmons.'

For a moment Lorna was taken aback. Since her arrival
in Portugal she had kept up a desultory correspondence
with Derek, but his last letter had made no mention of a
visit to Portugal. What was he doing here now? Perhaps

there was bad news concerning her aunt? Regardless of Rafael's sardonic glance, she ran across the room and wrenched open the door.

'Derek! What on earth are you doing here?' With an eagerness she had never displayed to him before she caught him by the arm. 'Is anything the matter – when did you arrive?'

'Early this morning, and nothing's the matter. I just thought I'd take a holiday.' He placed an affectionate arm across her shoulder. 'I hope you don't mind me barging in like this.'

'Of course not! It's like a breath of home to see you again. For a moment I was afraid something had happened to Aunt Marion.' She led him into the drawing-room and his eyes flickered from her to the man standing by the fireplace.

With a murmur of apology Lorna introduced him. 'Derek, Senhor Rodriguez – my host. Senhor, a friend of mine from England.'

The two men shook hands.

'Are you Amalia's husband?' Derek asked.

'No, you are thinking of my cousin.' The Portuguese indicated a chair. 'Do sit down. How about a drink?'

'Thanks. Something long and cool.'

Calm and apparently unruffled, Rafael turned to the cocktail cabinet, and Lorna watched him helplessly, wondering if he were ever caught off guard. Passionately disturbed a moment ago, he was now dispensing drinks with the cool efficiency of a bartender.

She sighed and turned to Derek. 'Have you seen Aunt Marion lately?'

'We had dinner together the night before last. She sends her love and told me to tell you she's never written so many successful articles in her life, so you needn't hurry back!'

'That makes me miss her all the more! It seems a lifetime since I saw her!'

T—C

'Because you're a lady of leisure.' Derek grinned at Rafael. 'I hope you're not letting Lorna become lazy.'

'There's no chance of that. She is too busy interfering in other people's affairs to become lazy.'

There was an awkward pause and Lorna hurriedly turned to Derek. 'Are you staying long?"

'A couple of weeks.'

'Why didn't you write and tell me you were coming?'

'And spoil the surprise? Not likely! I took a chance that you'd be glad to see me.'

'I'm delighted. You've stopped me feeling homesick!' She smiled appraisingly at him, warming to the candour and generosity in his rugged, freckled face. Not good-looking by any stretch of the imagination, he had a homeliness about him that was immensely likable. Tall, loose-limbed, with a thatch of rough, red hair, he was the sort of man she would have liked as a brother.

'Are you staying at the Palace?'

His blue eyes crinkled. 'On my allowance? Have a heart, darling! I sorted out a small pension not far from here. There are only about five bedrooms, but it's clean and has all the mod. cons.!'

'We are not barbarians, Mr. Simmons,' Rafael put in. 'We have even civilized the weather!'

'Thank goodness for that! It's been freezing in London all the week.'

Lorna stood up, unable to tolerate this hollow exchange of platitudes.

'If you came here for the sun then you'd better come into the garden. Senhor Rodriguez was just going out and we mustn't detain him.'

'Right.' Derek finished his drink at a gulp; with a nod to Rafael followed Lorna down the terrace steps to the lawn.

'Phew!' he said when they were out of earshot. 'So that's the head of the family! No wonder you wanted to escape. How do you get on with him?'

'All right,' Lorna said guardedly. 'He's out most of the time.'

'Good.' He caught her hand. 'The less you see of him the better I'll be pleased. Damn it, Lorna, London isn't the same without you. How much longer are you going to stay here?'

'Until the baby comes.' Gently Lorna drew her hand away. 'Tell me all the news first. I seem to have been out of touch so long.'

'Everyone and everything is fine, but I refuse to talk about them at the moment. It's you I'm interested in.' He looked down at her and his voice trailed off.' Damn it, Lorna! I knew there was something different about you. You've cut your hair.'

'Do you like it?' She turned her head from side to side, and he pursed his lips dubiously.

'I don't know. It suits you, of course, but it makes you look different. Too glamorous.'

'Nonsense – you didn't notice it until it was right under you nose.'

'Is that so?' His arms stole round her waist and he tried to kiss her.

'Derek, don't! Someone might see.'

'Who cares? I don't mind if the whole world knows I love you.'

'Well, I do. Now behave yourself or I'll be sorry you came.'

'I'll wear down your resistance one day,' he threatened, 'and you'll have to give in. I only hope I won't die of shock when you finally say "I will".'

She burst out laughing. 'It'll be your own fault, then. You shouldn't be so persistent. Now come and see the pavilion – it's my favourite spot in the whole garden.'

As a pebble thrown into a pool, Derek's sudden appearance in Estoril cast ripples across the surface of the whole Rodriguez family. The Senhora treated Lorna with a cordiality amounting almost to affection and the two

Portuguese girls alternately teased and questioned her. Only Rafael behaved as if she had no physical existence at all, and apart from the conventional greetings barely addressed a single word to her. As the days passed Lorna found she could think more coherently about her discovery of the ring and decided to wait until she was able to leave Portugal before saying anything about it. Once the story was out it would be impossible to remain in the house, and as long as Amalia needed her she would keep silent.

Although her decision was made she still longed to shield Rafael and her mind was constantly occupied with ways and means of doing it.

One sultry night, unable to sleep, she decided to escape from her room and sit for a while in the cool of the pavilion. The soft, panther resonance of her footfalls on the grass only served to accentuate the silence around her, and like a row of eyes the windows watched her as she crossed the lawn.

She mounted the pavilion steps, pushed open the door and felt cautiously around for the switch. Light flooded the little room and she drew back with a stifled gasp. Lying on a wicker chair was the body of a girl, her thin legs bent awkwardly beneath her, the face gaunt and bloodless. Controlling herself with an effort, Lorna took a tentative step forward, letting out a sigh of relief as she saw the fingers of one hand uncurl. She bent and shook her gently by the shoulder.

Slowly the pale eyelids lifted and dolorous eyes gazed uncomprehendingly into Lorna's.

'Qem é a Senhora? O que quer?'

'Thank God you're alive!' Lorna was too upset to care whether she was being understood or not.

'Did I frighten you?' The girl spoke English with ease and assurance. 'I'm sorry. For a moment I didn't – I couldn't make out where I was.'

Lorna's fear changed to anger. 'You've no business to

be here at all! This is private land. It belongs to the Rodriguez family and—'.

'You needn't go on,' the girl said wearily. 'I know all about it. It's just that this was always my favourite spot.'

'What do you mean? Who are you?'

'Rosalia. Perhaps you've heard of me.'

'Rosalia!' Lorna sank down on the chair. 'Rafael's sister!'

'Yes. But who are you—his wife?'

Lorna blushed. 'No, I'm a friend of Amalia's.'

'So she married Manoel after all. I wondered if she would. What is she doing here?'

'She's come home to have a baby. They live in Brazil now, you know.'

'I didn't, but never mind. The only news I've heard was of Papa's death.' Her voice grew tremulous. 'But how is my mother? Is she well? I've longed to see her and speak to her.'

'Come up to the house, then. It's quite simple.'

'I wish it were. But you can't turn back the clock no matter how much you want to.' The girl stood up and pulled her shabby coat about her. 'I never thought my family would be too proud to see me because I married Frank instead of Juan.'

'Perhaps it was more than that. I mean—I mean,' Lorna felt her way carefully, 'they might have forgiven you if you'd told them in the first place. Perhaps if you'd spoken to your father . . .'

'Nothing would have made Papa change his mind.'

'I know, but—' Lorna twisted her hands together. 'Perhaps if you'd seen your parents *after* you were married.'

'I intended to, but Frank changed his plans and we left for Australia as soon as the ceremony was over. I wrote and begged Papa to forgive me and kept on writing until I was taken ill and went into hospital.'

'And when you came out again?'

'I made up my mind to forget them. I too am a Rodriguez.'

'But you've come back now?'

Rosalia averted her head. 'Because my husband is dead. He was killed in an accident a year ago.' She rubbed her eyes childishly. 'You are a stranger, yet I'm talking to you as I have to no one else.'

'Perhaps it's because we are strangers,' Lorna said quietly.

There was a pause. Rosalia said nothing and after a moment Lorna began again. 'Why didn't you come home sooner, senhora?'

Still the girl did not reply. Then after a moment she held out her hands and shrugged. 'How silly of me – I was almost too proud to tell you the reason. But I should remember that poor people can't afford to have pride – and I was certainly poor! Frank gambled: it was in his blood and he couldn't stop.'

'And his death. How did it happen?'

'Saving a little girl from getting run over. He managed to pull the child out of the way, but the lorry struck him instead.'

'How dreadful for you!'

Rosalia's eyes filled with tears. 'For a few months I didn't know what to do. It's difficult to be in a strange country without any money or friends.'

'If only you'd written to your mother. I'm sure she would have helped you.'

'I was determined to come home under my own steam, and I certainly did. I washed so many greasy dishes I still dream of it at night!' She flexed her hands, the fingers hard, the small palms calloused. 'Do you know, I cried more over spoiling my hands than anything else. Just shows how vain women can be.'

'You've been marvellous. When I think how you've suffered . . .' Lorna stood up. 'Let's go to the house. Your mother will be overjoyed to see you.'

'No – no.' Rosalia drew back. 'Wait a little. I can't go now. Not yet. I seem to have lost my courage.'

'But you haven't come half way across the world to give up at the last minute.'

'I know, but I don't think I can face them.' Her voice trembled and tears coursed down her cheeks. 'Suppose they won't forgive me, that they blame me for my father's death? You're a stranger – I can't expect you to understand everything that happened, but—'

'I do, I do!' Lorna caught the girl's arm. 'Please don't think I'm unsympathetic. I'm not, and I'll do anything I can to help you.' She paused, desperately wondering how to begin. 'I think there's something you ought to know first – something I ought to tell you. You'll probably tell me to mind my own business and you're right – but I can't stand by and see you suffer for a crime you didn't commit.'

'What do you mean? I don't understand you.'

Lorna twisted her hands tightly together. 'Your parents – your father – didn't refuse to see you because you eloped. It was much more serious than that.'

'What other reason could there have been?'

Lorna swallowed. 'They thought you were a thief!'

'How *dare* you say such a thing to me?' Rosalia drew herself up to her full height. 'A Rodriguez would rather starve than steal! You must be mad!'

'I'm not, I'm telling you the truth. You've got to believe me.'

'But what could I have stolen? My clothes, my silver hairbrushes, my—'

'Much more than that,' Lorna interposed desperately. 'Your ring!'

For a moment Rosalia stared at her uncomprehendingly, then the colour drained from her face, leaving it sickly grey.

'No, no, it's not true!' Her voice was strangled. 'I didn't steal it – I gave it back. I couldn't return it to Juan myself, but I left it with a note. I asked him to deliver it for me – to see he got it. I never thought – never doubted – oh, my God!' She put her hand to her throat and without another word slid forward to the ground.

Lorna bent over the inert body and pulled it on to the chair: automatically she unbuttoned the collar and rubbed the limp hands. Rosalia's last words had confirmed all her fears; there could be no further proof of Rafael's guilt.

Slowly the girl stirred and opened her eyes. A low moan escaped her lips and Lorna leaned forward.

'Don't take it so badly,' she implored. 'It isn't your fault. I wouldn't have told you if I'd known you'd be so upset. Here, take my handkerchief and wipe your eyes and then come up to the house.'

'No, no! I can't – not now.'

'Of course you can. There's nothing to stop you.'

'I won't, I tell you, I won't! You can't make me!' Her voice rose on a scream and Lorna hushed her as if she were a child.

'I won't make you do anything. There's no need to get so excited. Only I can't see the point in your coming home if you're going to run away again.'

'But I can't go through with it,' Rosalia cried. 'I can't, I tell you! Not now I know he's a thief.' She was shaken by a fresh bout of sobbing, and Lorna put her arms around her placatingly.

'Don't cry, Rosalia. You needn't come back if you don't want to do so.'

'It isn't that,' the girl hiccoughed. 'It's just that I can't take it all in. He was always so kind and gentle to me. Even though we quarrelled sometimes I never thought he'd be a common thief. Never!'

'Well, it won't help you to stay out here. You've got to face up to things some time. You're innocent and it isn't fair to take someone else's guilt.'

'But don't you see it's my fault? If I hadn't asked him to help me he wouldn't have been tempted.'

'It's silly to say that. You weren't to know what he'd do. Now please, Rosalia, let me take you to your mother.'

'No.' The girl set her lips. 'I'm not being hysterical or childish, but I can't go home tonight. Everything has altered and I must have a few days to think things out.'

'You can do that at home.'

'I've got to work it out alone.' Rosalia dragged herself to her feet, her face still deathly pale. 'I shouldn't have come back. They hate me enough as it is.'

'They don't!'

'They do! Rafael would kill me if he had the chance. Well, he won't get it – I'll rob him of that pleasure.'

'That's a silly way to talk.' Lorna was becoming angry. 'You're not a coward to take the easy way out. And anyway, why should you sacrifice yourself for him?'

'Haven't you ever cared for someone so much that you'd do anything not to harm them?'

Across the small interior of the white pavilion the two girls faced one another, and it was Lorna who turned away first.

'I'm not sure. A week ago I might have said no, but now I can't answer you.' She touched Rosalia's arm. 'But that's still no excuse for doing anything foolish. You've got to be strong enough to face facts even if they're unpalatable ones.'

'You sound like a preacher!'

'I'm sorry, but it's the truth. Now let's be practical. Where are you going to stay?'

'Anywhere. Don't worry about me.'

'I won't let you leave here alone, you're not in a fit state. I've got a friend staying in Estoril who might be able to help us. Perhaps he'll find you a room in his hotel.' She stood up. 'Wait for me here I won't be a minute.'

She tiptoed through the hall to the library and dialled Derek's number. The porter at the other end kept exclaiming that he could not hear, but Lorna was afraid to raise her voice above a whisper and with difficulty managed to explain that she wanted to speak to the Englishman.

After a moment Derek came on the line, his voice sharp with concern.

'What's the matter? Is anything wrong?'

'No, no. Not to me. But I'd like to see you right away. Can you come over?'

'You mean now? Tonight?'

'Yes. It's urgent.' She looked fearfully at the door. 'I can't explain here. I'll be waiting for you at the pavilion Be as quick as you can.'

The next half hour dragged past on leaden feet. Rosalia started nervously at every sound, her fear of discovery communicating itself to Lorna, who peered anxiously out through the pavilion door every few minutes. At last she heard footsteps on the gravel path and sped down the steps to greet Derek.

He caught her hand in a painful grip. 'Thank God you're all right! For a moment I was afraid ...'

'But I said nothing was wrong with me. It's – it's Rosalia – Rafael's sister!' In an undertone she told him the facts. Her discovery of the ring, her reasons for believing that Rafael was the miscreant and finally her finding Rosalia in the pavilion.

When she had finished Derek still looked mystified. 'But what do you want me to do?'

'Take Rosalia to your pension. She absolutely refuses to go up to the house and I'm afraid to let her go anywhere alone. She might ...'

'I see.' He sighed. 'It's a hell of a problem, isn't it? Still, I'm glad you had the sense to call me, although I can't quite see what good it will do to hide her.'

'I don't want to hide her. I just want to see she's all

right for one night. I'm sure she'll see things differently in the morning.'

'I hope so.' He straightened his shoulders. 'Well, I'll take her back with me. The dining-room isn't full, if that's anything to go by.'

Lorna heaved a sigh of relief and preceded Derek up the pavilion steps and introduced him to Rosalia. Although slow to react, once he had time to absorb the facts Derek, like the true Englishman he was, acted coolly and efficiently. Wrapping Rosalia in a warm coat, he picked up her pitifully small valise and bustled her to where a taxi was waiting at the front gate.

'I picked it up on the way,' he whispered to Lorna, 'because I thought you were going to do a bunk! But it's certainly come in handy.'

The car was moving off when he thrust his head out of the window. 'Don't worry, darling, everything will be all right. See you in the morning.'

Lorna walked back to the house. The crescent moon was poised above the tall thin chimney and the garden was mysteriously alive with patches of light and shade. Its heartbreaking loveliness served only to accentuate her misery. With a sigh she crossed the hall, drawing back with a start as a light went on and Rafael stepped out of the shadows. In a maroon dressing-gown faced with gold, his dark hair sleek and unruffled, he barred her way at the top of the stairs.

'What were you doing in the garden, Miss Fairfax?'

'Walking.'

'At this hour? Surely you could find a more reasonable time?'

'I didn't think it mattered. Next time I'll let you know if I go out after hours.'

'There's no need to do that,' he said coldly. 'Your movements are no concern of mine.'

'Thank you, señor, that's what I thought.' She tried to walk past him, but he refused to move out of the way.

'One other thing, Miss Fairfax. May I suggest there are better times for a rendezvous than at midnight?'

Lorna's eyes dilated with fear and Rafael misinterpreted the look.

'Don't worry,' he said scornfully. 'I am not in the habit of spying. I merely heard voices and got up to investigate.'

Lorna's relief was so great that a fine veil of perspiration covered her forehead. 'I'm sorry you were disturbed for nothing, senhor. Now if you'll excuse me . . .'

'Not until I've finished. I'm glad I heard you, if only to give you timely warning. I am sure there is no danger in meeting your English friend at such a time – your countrymen are notoriously cold lovers – but it is bad for your reputation to be seen wandering about the grounds late at night.'

'I don't think my reputation is any concern of yours.'

'I must disagree with you on that point. When you are in my house you must behave as I would expect a guest to behave. What you do when in your own country is your business, but if you wish to remain with Amalia you must conform to the habits of my countrywomen.'

'I was not aware that I had done anything to which you could take offence. My friendship with Mr. Simmons is perfectly innocent.'

'From what I know of Mr. Simmons I am not in the least surprised!'

She caught her breath sharply. 'Really, senhor, you're insufferable! As you seem to dislike me so much I'm surprised you bother about me.'

For a long moment he was silent. 'There is more than a grain of truth in what you have said. In the future I will not waste my time with you.'

'Is that all you have to say?'

'It is enough, I think.'

'So do I. Good night, senhor.'

Without another word she slipped past him and ran

down the corridor to her room. Trembling, she undressed and climbed into bed, but it was impossible to sleep. Memories of Rosalia's return filled her mind. What did the future hold for Rafael now? She could not imagine his accepting any change in his status. With his money and power he would surely be able to gloss over everything. The ring would be returned to its rightful owner and an excuse fabricated for its disappearance. Only a few people would know the truth, and with all her heart Lorna wished she was not one of them.

CHAPTER FIVE

THE following morning Amalia decided to go shopping and Lorna dutifully accompanied her friend down to the town. The shops in Estoril were built in two semi-circular arcades, one on each side of the Casino gardens that stretched from the top of the hill almost to the promenade. The choice of articles was not as wide as in Lisbon and far more expensive, but the price did not concern Amalia, who chose some exquisite cambric handkerchiefs with fine Portuguese lace edging, and a bedjacket in the same delicate handwork.

'It's beautiful.' Lorna admired the cobweb patterns, marvelling that hands could have made them.

'Machine-made lace is more the vogue now. It's cheaper and stronger.'

'A machine couldn't make anything as perfect as these.'

'Perhaps not.' Amalia spoke in rapid Portuguese to the girl behind the counter and then turned back to Lorna. 'I've asked her to send the things up to the house, but these are yours.' She slipped a packet of handkerchiefs into Lorna's hand.

'Amalia, I couldn't! They're much too expensive.'

'Don't be silly. If I couldn't afford it I wouldn't do it.'

Still protesting, Lorna followed her friend out of the shop and stood beside her on the pavement, protected from the sun by the arcade.

'How about a drink before we go back to the house? I must treat you to something in return for such a lovely present.'

'Done. I'll have the most expensive cake I can find! Where shall we sit? It looks rather crowded.' Amalia waved a hand to the small tables and chairs that filled the arcade from one end to the other, making the shops almost inaccessible.

'There's a table free outside Cook's office. I'll lead the way. Call me if you get stuck.'

Lorna forced a passage through the crowd of sun-tanned holidaymakers, the women in bright summer frocks, the men in open-necked shirts. She longed to know what was happening to Rosalia and Derek, but one look at her friend's beaming face as they sat down at the table told her she must contain her impatience a little longer.

'I feel as if I've been out of circulation for years,' Amalia said as she beckoned to the waiter. 'I felt I just had to get out this morning.'

'A good idea, or I wouldn't have met you.'

They turned in surprise to see Derek standing in front of Cook's doorway. 'What are you doing in town so early?' he asked.

'Shopping,' Amalia grinned. 'It's the only thing that will get me up!'

'Just like a woman – they're the same the world over!' He came over to the table. 'Mind if I join you?'

'Not at all. Do sit down and tell me what you think of Portugal.'

'It's perfect! The scenery, the food, everything.'

'Including Lorna?'

'How did you guess?'

'Were you booking your passage home?' Lorna put in quickly.

He nodded. 'I had a telegram from the office this morning which means I'll have to get back by the end of next week. The boss doesn't know the meaning of the word "holiday".'

The waiter came up with a tray of gateaux and as Amalia concentrated on the cream puffs and éclairs, Derek spoke to Lorna in an undertone.

'I've left her at the hotel, still fast asleep, and told the maid to stay with her. What are you going to do? We can't keep her hidden for long.'

'I know. We'll have to persuade her to go home.'

'Why not tell the Senhora? It's her responsibility.'

'I can't. I promised—'

'Damn it, Lorna, you can't let Rodriguez get away with it. He deserves to face the consequences.'

'We can't talk now,' she said hurriedly. 'I'll meet you back here in an hour.'

'All right, but I won't let you—'

'What are you two whispering about?' Amalia interrupted. 'Or would it embarrass me to know?'

'Not at all,' Derek said with aplomb. 'We were admiring your figure!'

'What a wonderful lie! I'll know better than to ask you next time. Choose your cake, Lorna, before he eats them all.'

The next half-hour passed in idle chatter, and Lorna was fretting with impatience by the time they said goodbye to Derek and began the slow walk up the hill to the house. Amalia was too busy talking about the nurse she had engaged to notice her friend's lack of interest, and she was surprised when Lorna stopped at the entrance to the drive.

'I won't come in if you don't mind. I think I'll take another walk.'

'Why didn't you say so in the first place?' Amalia grinned. 'You could have stayed with Derek instead of dragging all the way up the hill with me.'

Lorna bit back a denial. 'You jump to conclusions too quickly,' she said lightly. 'It isn't Derek so much as the fact that he's a breath of home.'

'That's your excuse and you're sticking to it! But I don't mind: 'I'll have the last laugh on you yet!' With a wave Amalia walked towards the house and Lorna hared back the way she had come.

Derek was still sitting at the table and she slipped into the seat beside him.

'You were quick.'

'I ran all the way.'

'Poor darling, you look upset. I hope you're not worrying too much.'

'No, but—'

'It's not your problem, Lorna,' he said sternly, 'and the quicker you realize it the better. As I said before, if Rosalia won't tell her mother the truth then you've got to do it.'

'How can I? It isn't my affair.'

'Exactly what I said in the first place,' he was triumphant. 'If it isn't your affair then let Rosalia do what the hell she likes. If she's fool enough to let her brother get away with it serve her right.' He shot her a keen glance. 'It's what you want deep down, anyway.'

'What do you mean?'

'That you're fond of the man.'

'You're letting your imagination run away with you.' The smile did not quite reach her eyes. 'I never thought you were so fanciful, Derek. It was part of your charm that you were so—'

'Stodgy,' he finished for her, and caught her hand. 'Poor darling you, were never very good at concealing your feelings, especially from me. I know you think me a dull dog, but I've been hoping that absence might have made your heart grow fonder.'

'I *am* fond of you, Derek. Very fond.'

'I hate that word. It means so little — and I want so much.' He looked down at her hand, her tanned fingers inert and resting almost reluctantly in his. 'I'm going to keep pestering you, Lorna. I refuse to take no for an answer.'

'It would be much simpler if you could,' she said quietly, and looking up stared directly into Rafael's eyes. He was in his open roadster, the nose of the bonnet almost touching the table. Quickly she disengaged her hand from Derek's. 'There's Rafael!'

Derek looked up and saluted. 'Come and have a drink.'

'Afraid not, I am on my way to Lisbon.'

'Just one for the road then?'

Rafael glanced round for the waiter. 'I am sorry, I'm afraid I cannot wait. The man is busy and I am in a hurry. If you will excuse me I will have a drink with you another time.' He moved to start the car and then as an afterthought, turned back. 'By the way, Simmons, you should be more considerate of Lorna's bright eyes — they are red-rimmed from lack of sleep.' Punctiliously he nodded to them, climbed into the car and drove off.

Derek looked mystified. 'What did he mean by *that* cryptic remark?'

'He heard our voices in the garden last night and when I crossed the hall he was waiting for me.'

'Good. It'll show him he doesn't own you. I don't like the way he looks at you, Lorna.'

'No one owns me!' she said tartly. 'You're imagining things.'

'Don't lose your temper, old girl. You're too touchy about Rodriguez. Let's change the subject.'

During the next few days Lorna visited Rosalia frequently and tried to cajole her to return home. Each time the girl flatly refused. Reluctantly Lorna accepted the position. It was like living on the edge of a volcano. Every day increased the strain of waiting and her body trembled when Rafael spoke in the aloof, icy tones he now used to her.

Inez's sudden arrival at the house did not improve the position. It was the first time Lorna had seen her since her own precipitate flight from the Castro house in Algarve, and one afternoon when she encountered the Portuguese girl on the stairs she offered an apology for her behaviour.

'You must have thought me awfully rude, Miss Castro, leaving your parents' home the way I did.'

Inez lifted her shoulders expressively. In an amber-coloured dress, she looked more than ever like a tawny cat. 'My parents thought it strange, but I didn't. It is what I would have expected of you.'

'Meaning?'

'That you do not understand the Portuguese temperament. Only an Englishwoman would have jumped to the conclusion that Amalia was broken-hearted because Manoel went away for the weekend.'

'She was.'

'Because she is highly strung at the moment.' Inez moved up a step until she was looking down on Lorna. 'I believe I told you once before that you can never truly understand the way we Portuguese women feel. A woman should be capable of holding her husband's interest all the time. If she is not then she deserves to be left alone.'

'What a cruel thing to say! It is quite obvious you speak from lack of experience.'

'And what experience do you have?' Inez said tartly.

'English women don't believe in experience.' Unbeknown Rafael had come down the corridor, his crêpe-soled shoes making no sound on the marble floor. 'May I enquire what you are talking about? It sounded most interesting.'

Inez linked her arm in his and gave him a wide smile. 'You would be bored if I told you. Is that not so, Miss Fairfax?'

'You should know better than I. You have just told me I have no experience of men.'

Rafael looked amused. 'This sounds like a typical woman's conversation! Was Inez baiting you?'

Lorna bit her lip. 'Possibly, senhor. But I trust I did not rise to the hook.' With a murmur of excuse she moved past and went on her way upstairs.

This was only the first of many skirmishes with Inez.

With the Portuguese girl's ability to hurt, the web of antagonism became insupportable and Lorna could feel the delicate fabric of surface appearances crumbling. The climax occurred one Friday evening when they were all sitting in the drawing-room drinking coffee. Sipping hers, Lorna reflected how little Derek knew when he said the Rodriguez family were not her concern. She was inextricably bound because of her love for Rafael. She sighed and set down her coffee cup. It was no good denying it any longer; even the knowledge that he was a thief could not stop her from worshipping him, from wanting him with every fibre of her being and knowing that if he wanted her she would not have the power to resist him.

'You are very quiet, Miss Fairfax,' Inez broke into her reverie. 'Could it be that you are thinking of your fair-haired Englishman?'

'No, it couldn't,' Lorna replied with unusual sharpness. 'And would you kindly refrain from calling him *my* Englishman? He is merely a friend.'

'There is no need to be shy. All the world loves a lover.'

Lorna's eyes flashed and Amalia said quickly : 'Don't bait Lorna, Inez. She doesn't like being teased. I don't like it when Manoel teases me either.'

Manoel sighed. 'Now what is the matter? Women are so difficult to please. If you tease them they object and if you don't they think you're in love with someone else! What can one do to satisfy such fickle creatures?'

In the general laughter Lorna glanced surreptitiously at her watch. Rosalia would begin to get restless if she delayed her nightly visit any longer.

She stood up. 'Will you excuse me – I promised to meet Derek at his hotel and I'm late.'

'Going anywhere special?' Amalia enquired.

'To the Casino,' she lied. 'We've never been.'

'Then it's time you improved your education,' Manoel said suavely. 'There's a good cabaret on at the moment. I wouldn't mind seeing it again.'

'Not tonight,' his wife said sharply. 'You promised you'd stay with me.'

'Of course, my love, I had no intention of going.'

With a murmured good night Lorna walked to the door.

'You have forgotten your bag, Miss Fairfax.' Rafael spoke from his seat in the corner, and Lorna turned blindly, fumbling for it on the chair. It opened and the contents spilled over the floor.

"Allow me.' He bent and picked up the powder puff, keys and lipstick, placing them in her bag and slowly snapping the clasp. 'If you're going to the Casino with your friend I can take you. Inez and I are going too.'

'I promised I'd call for Derek at eight.'

'Then you'd better wait for us, it is nearly that now. He should call for you,' he said beneath his breath, 'or perhaps that is not your custom.' He turned to Inez. 'Run upstairs and get your wrap, my dear. We can give Miss Fairfax a lift.'

Inez left the room and Manoel extended his arm to Amalia. 'It's too warm in here, my love. A little stroll in the garden will do you good.'

In dismay Lorna realized she was alone with Rafael and the air was electric with antagonism.

'When you have quite finished studying the carpet,' he said sarcastically, 'you can perhaps start on the ceiling. There are at least a thousand objects in this room you would rather look at than me.'

'Please,' she said breathlessly, 'don't bait me. I can't bear it.'

'And what have you been doing to me these last few weeks?'

'I – I don't know what you mean,' she faltered.

'Don't you? Are you so besotted with love for this Derek of yours that—'

'Leave Derek alone! He's got nothing to do with it.'

'So now I mustn't speak his name,' he said savagely. 'Is he too precious for me to talk about?'

'No, no, you're wrong, quite wrong! There's no point in arguing, I've made up my mind.'

'To marry him, I suppose? What an ideal couple you will make; both so cold and reserved!'

She turned on him angrily. 'Don't be too sure of that! We may not be so glib with our compliments or wear our hearts on our sleeves, but we're as warm as — as—'

'As this?'

For the second time since she had know him he pulled her into his arms, but now there was no tenderness in his kiss, only a brutal passion that overwhelmed her with its force.

She struggled to free herself, beating her hands against his back, but her frenzy only served to increase his ardour and he held her more closely, bruising her lips. Deliberately he caressed her, his hands moving over her back, down her hips, across her throat to her breasts. With a gasp she wrenched herself free, the flimsy material of her bodice tearing underneath his hands.

'You beast!' she gasped. 'You hateful beast!'

Sardonically Rafael regarded her, his eyes lingering on her flushed face and the curve of her breast where the material gaped.

'Passion suits you,' he said cruelly. 'I have never seen you look more – exciting. A pity I have made other plans.'

'Go on, senhor.' A wave of blackness advanced and receded in front of her eyes. 'I'm waiting to see how much lower you can stoop.'

'It is not stooping to take someone else's woman in your arms or to steal kisses that don't belong to you.'

Her hand flashed out and caught him a stinging blow across the face. 'Stealing should come easily to a thief like you! But I wouldn't be as easy to keep as the emerald!'

'What are you talking about?' He shook her violently by the shoulders. 'What do you know of the emerald?'

'Everything!' She threw back her head and stared at him defiantly. 'I know everything.' She was sick and dizzy with the force of his shaking, but she refused to give in. 'You can't frighten me with your strength, Senhor Rodriguez. The truth will come out in the end no matter what happens. Rosalia and Derek will tell everyone what you've done.'

As suddenly as he had caught hold of her he let her go. 'This has gone far enough. For God's sake tell me what you're talking about before I lose my temper completely. What do you know of Rosalia? Where is she?'

'At Derek's hotel. She's – she's been there nearly a week.' Lorna clung to the back of a chair, gasping for breath. 'I found the emerald in your drawer when I came back from Algarve. I was looking for some cards and found – and found the ring. It wasn't difficult to piece the story together after that.'

'I see.' His voice was controlled and venomous. 'It is much clearer now. I must admit I never expected you to show quite so much cunning. But why were you keeping my sister hidden? What was the purpose in waiting so long before accusing me, or did you intend to resort to blackmail?'

She said nothing, and he moved a step nearer. Never had she seen a man so moved by fury. It was as if a mask had dropped from his face and she was looking into his very soul.

'At this moment I could enjoy strangling you,' he said slowly. 'I never believed I could loathe anyone as I loathe you. But I've nothing to say to you now. Go down to the hotel with Luiz and bring Rosalia back immediately. It is time a lot of things were cleared up.' He turned away. 'Get out, Lorna. Get out while I can still control myself!'

Unable to think ahead, Lorna fled to her room, changed her dress and ran down the stairs to find the chauffeur. Matters were out of her hands now and nothing could hide the truth any longer.

After one look at Lorna's face Rosalia knew it was useless to argue. Desolately she packed her bag and climbed into the Cadillac, silent as they drove up the hill to the pink house.

All the family were assembled in the library when the two girls entered and the Senhora took a step towards them.

'Rosalia!'

With a sob the girl flung herself into her mother's arms, and the silence of the room was punctuated by broken words of endearment as they clung together. Amalia made a movement, but Manoel restrained her and she subsided in her chair, her eyes large and luminous. Only Rafael ignored the situation as he stood at his desk, his long, tapering fingers opening and closing a green leather box.

Lorna stood hesitantly at the door, longing to escape yet unwilling to leave Rosalia to the mercy of the man at the desk, a man with strained face and burning eyes.

'Sit down, Rosalia,' Rafael rapped out. 'You will have plenty of time with Mother when this is all over.' He looked at Lorna with distaste. 'For your benefit I will begin at the beginning. As you know *so much* it is a pity not to acquaint you with the whole story.' He closed his eyes for a moment as if to control himself and when he opened them again his face was completely blank, as if he were recounting a tale in which he had no part. 'It began three years ago when Rosalia eloped. Pointless to go over the anger and humiliation that resulted from her action, anger which changed to horror when we discovered she had not returned her engagement ring to Juan Diniz.'

'That's not true!' Rosalia interrupted.

'Be quiet!' her brother said sharply. 'Hear me out first. It is the least you can do. Immediately we learned the news I followed my sister and her husband to Australia, but it was nearly two months before I could trace them. I had never realized that a continent could be so large nor that two people could be swallowed up as if they had never existed. By the time I found them, Rosalia was in hospital and her husband informed me that she did not wish to see me.'

'I didn't say that,' Rosalia cried. 'I never refused to see you. I never even knew you were there!'

'I see. Well, it does not affect the story.' For the first time Rafael looked directly at his sister, the lines on either side of his mouth deepening with bitterness. 'If I had not remembered the happy childhood we shared, if I could have forgotten so many things about you that I once loved, I would have had you and your husband arrested. But I was a fool – I came home without doing anything. Frank –' his contempt for the man was implicit in the name – 'Frank refused to discuss the ring or what he had done with it, and no amount of money on my part would make him give it up. I did not know at the time that it had already been sold. I came home and shortly after-wards Father died. I swore then that I would never speak your name again, but unfortunately Miss Fairfax ren-dered that impossible when she accused me earlier this evening of having stolen the ring myself.'

'And you did,' Lorna said loudly, unable to restrain herself any longer. 'You can't get away with lies, I won't let you! Rosalia's innocent and you know it. For good-ness' sake, Rosalia, tell them the truth. How can you sit there and keep quiet?' She ran across the room and caught the girl's hand. 'Please, darling, tell them what you told me in the pavilion. Tell them that you asked Rafael to give the ring back for you.'

'I didn't, I didn't!' Rosalia screamed. 'Why don't you leave me alone? Why must you torment me like this?' She pulled away from Lorna, the harsh sound of her sobs filling the room. 'Why must you make me admit that my

husband was a thief? That he made a fool of me as he did
of everyone else? Until you came along I at least had pity
for him. Now you've taken even that away from me.' She
sank down on the floor, her voice so low that it could
barely be heard across the full length of the room. 'How
could you be so stupid as to think I'd give the ring to
Rafael? He would have guessed immediately that something was wrong. I gave it to Frank – to Frank, I tell you!
He promised to return it to Juan the day we eloped. I
didn't know that—'

'*Comos Diabos!* Will I never get to the bottom of
this?' In two strides Rafael was at his sister's side and
hoisted her none too gently to her feet. 'For heaven's sake
don't ramble on, Rosalia. What are you trying to say?'

'Don't you know?' she whispered. 'Isn't it clear?'

'It is not,' he grated. 'I can't make head or tail of it.'
He shook her again. 'Come, Rosalia, begin from the
beginning. You owe us that at least.'

Rosalia moistened her lips. 'I – I left the ring with
Frank – I've just told you. We'd arranged not to meet
the last two days in case you – anyone – suspected our
plans. But we had a secret trysting place at the back of
the pavilion and we left notes for each other every day.
That's where I put the ring. I left it with a letter asking
Frank to leave it for me at the Diniz house before we
eloped.' She paused. 'I'd no idea he hadn't done so until
I came back here and saw Lorna. That's why I couldn't
face you. I had to have time to think things out.'

'Why?'

'Because I couldn't believe there was nothing left of my
marriage except bitterness and wasted years.' With a
visible effort Rosalia controlled her trembling, but when
she continued she kept her eyes firmly on the ground. 'I'm
not asking you to forgive me. You can say "I told you so"
and you're perfectly right. I know now that even the first
happy months Frank and I had together were built on
lies and deceit. But that doesn't alter the fact that I loved

him when I married him — that I loved a liar and a thief!
I've nothing left now. No husband, no family—'

'Don't say that!' Rafael broke in. 'You *have* your
family again, *querida*.' With indescribable tenderness he
drew Rosalia into his arms, and brother and sister stood
close together, everything forgotten in the joy of their
reunion.

After a moment he drew back. 'There are still one or
two other things to be said, *cara*, then we need never talk
of this — this episode again.' His eyes searched for Lorna
and when he spoke it was directly to her. 'Six months ago
I discovered to whom the ring had been sold. The man
who had bought it had known the jewel was a stolen one,
and it took a great deal of persuasion to convince him I
wouldn't call in the police the moment I had the ring in
my possession. Luckily he did believe me, and the
emerald arrived the day we left for Algarve. Unfortunately it was too late for me to return it to Senhor Diniz
then, so I put it in the bottom of my desk to await my
return. It is now safely with the other emeralds in the
Diniz collection. That is the whole story, and there I
think the matter ends.'

He turned back to his sister, and Lorna sank down on
a chair. How could she have misjudged Rafael so completely? How could she have been so stupid not to have
gone to him with her discovery, not to have asked him for
an explanation before jumping to her own conclusions?
With a start she realized he was speaking to her again.

'I think we should drink a toast to you, Miss Fairfax.
But for your unquenchable thirst for knowledge and discovery the whole truth might never have been known.'

Dimly she was aware that the maid had entered with
champagne and glasses and she watched as Rafael
poured out the sparkling wine and handed each member
of the family a glass. When he came to Lorna he stopped.

'You are astute, Miss Fairfax,' he said icily, 'but in
your excitement you forgot that two and two never make

five! Next time you should be more careful before con-
demning a man without a hearing.' He drained his glass
and threw the crystal goblet into the empty grate, shatter-
ing it into a thousand pieces.'

CHAPTER SIX

RAFAEL was alone in the library when Lorna knocked on the door later that evening.

'I'd like to talk to you, Rafael.'

'There is nothing for you to say.'

'But there is.' She closed the door and leant against it to hide her trembling. 'I want to explain – to apologize.'

'For calling me a thief or for thinking me one?'

She threw out her hand. 'You're perfectly right to be bitter. I'd feel the same if I were you. But you must understand – must try and imagine how I felt.'

The words rushed out in a torrent, defying him to interrupt as hurriedly, incoherently, she told him everything that had happened. Suddenly there was nothing more to say, and in an agony of suspense she waited for him to speak.

'I do not blame you,' he said at last. 'You were at perfect liberty to think what you liked. That I thought better of you was my mistake; stupidly I deluded myself into believing that you trusted me.' He moved nearer to his desk and the lamp threw a shadow on the tight line of his mouth. 'A Rodriguez is not used to being suspected, Miss Fairfax. You should know that by this time. Now if you will excuse me, I have some work to do.'

He bent his head over some papers, but she ignored the rebuff and came quickly across the carpet. 'Rafael,' her voice was a mere thread of sound and she coughed and began again. 'Rafael, I know you're still angry. Don't deny it, I can see it in your eyes.'

He looked up then, his expression mocking. 'Really, Miss Fairfax, I can assure you I'm not one whit angry with you, only with myself for having thought better of you.'

'That's a cruel thing to say! You're angry because I

misjudged you, yet that's exactly what you did to Rosalia.'

'I was entitled to. She is my sister.'

'That makes it all the worse!'

'On the contrary! If you had accused me of stealing anything but the ring—' he broke off. '*Diabos!* It is unthinkable that you believe me capable of harming my sister.'

'But I fought against it!' she cried. 'I tried with all my heart to believe you innocent, but everything was against you. Even Rosalia made matters worse. Can't you see that?'

'No,' he said coldly. 'You should have come and asked me for the truth.'

'I was afraid.'

'That I would confirm your fears? Or silence them with murder, perhaps?' She caught her breath and he shrugged. 'You are transparent, Miss Fairfax, it makes you uninteresting to talk to. Now please go. Believe me, I will only hurt you more if you stay.'

'Is that all you have to say?'

'Did you expect anything more?'

'No – no, I didn't. Not a thing.' She turned away blindly. 'I'm sorry I bothered you.'

Some fifteen minutes later she entered the lobby of the small pension to find Derek anxiously scanning the door.

'Lorna! I couldn't make out what had happened to you. What's the matter? You look all in.'

'I am. I wouldn't go through the last few hours for anything in the world.'

He drew her to a seat in the corner of the lounge and briefly she told him the news.

'Poor darling,' he said when she had finished, 'I wish I'd been there with you. It must have been awful.'

'It was.'

'Well, it's over now. Have a drink, you'll feel better for it.'

He signalled the waiter and then leaned back and surveyed her. 'So we were proved wrong after all! Somehow I didn't think Rodriguez was a thief.'

'You agreed with me at the time.'

'Because I let my jealousy blind me.' She said nothing, and he continued: 'But what happened when you accused him? I can't imagine him taking it lying down.'

'He didn't. He was furious. Not that I blame him. I was a fool not to have gone to him with the whole story in the first place.'

'It's easy to be wise after the event. At the time you were positive he was guilty. The best thing you can do is to return home with me. If he's going to be unpleasant—'

'There's no fear of that. Rafael's anger will merely take the form of ignoring me.'

'Equally unpleasant.' He leaned across towards her. 'There's no point in denying it, Lorna, Rodriguez can make it pretty uncomfortable for you, and my opinion is that you should come home. I'm sure Amalia would be the first to agree with me.'

'I've no intention of asking her. Please, Derek, we've gone over all this before.'

'I know, but I've a one-track mind as far as you're concerned, darling. I'm crazy about you – I—'

'Derek, no – not now.'

'Why? The Rodriguez family are nicely settled, or do you think I'm so stupid I don't know the *real* reason you keep putting me off? O.K., don't look so miserable, I know when I'm treading on thin ice.' He stood up. 'Come on. We might as well go to the Casino and try and forget our worries in the mad spin of the ball!'

Her smile was a little wan. 'A good idea. I think my luck might be in tonight!'

Gradually life readjusted itself. Rosalia was woven once more into the family pattern and Rafael's hostile

attitude to Lorna resolved itself into an armed neutrality.
In an effort to slough the membrance of pain and disillusionment Lorna turned her whole attention to
Amalia. As the hot, humid days of August gave way to
September the position between the young couple
deteriorated further, and after a particularly violent
quarrel Amalia stormed into her friend's room, hysteric-
ally screaming that she would run away the moment the
baby was born, a statement which Lorna heartily but
silently endorsed.

Yet although she tried to see the humorous side she was
forced to admit there was nothing she could do, and she
sat one afternoon in the garden turning the problem over
in her mind. The grass was brown and withered and the
flowers drooped under the white glare that beat down
relentlessly from early morning until the quick descent of
dusk.

She closed her eyes for a moment and when she woke
her throat was parched and dry. Glancing down at her
watch, she was startled to see she had slept for several
hours. Hurriedly she got to her feet, but the garden began
to revolve alarmingly and she steadied herself on the arm
of her chair and rubbed her hand across her forehead; it
was wet with perspiration. She took a step towards the
house and faltered. Dark spots expanded until they
seemed to burst in her brain; jagged streaks of light
flashed across the horizon and with every step a feeling of
nausea grew stronger. She tottered across the lawn to the
foot of the terrace, dimly aware of the figure of a man
above her.

'What were you doing in the garden, Miss Fairfax?'
Rafael spoke curtly. 'I thought I told you not to go out in
the sun without a hat.'

'I know. It was stupid of me.' Her tongue was so
swollen she could hardly speak. 'I didn't realize it was so
strong.'

'The sun is always strong in summer. I noticed you on

the lawn earlier, but I thought you'd have enough sense to come in.'

'I meant to, but I – I fell asleep – I hadn't realized I was – was there so long.'

Holding tightly to the railing, she climbed the steps, and as she came into focus he noticed her face.

'*Diabos*, you're like a ghost! What is it? Are you ill?'

She swayed. 'No – yes, I – I think it's the sun.'

She opened her mouth to speak, but no words came, and silently she crumpled at his feet.

For the next few days Lorna lay in a darkened room unconscious of her surroundings. She was aware only of an unquenchable thirst in a dark sea of pain. Voices soothed but could not placate her and she tossed and turned fretfully, throwing off the covering sheets in an effort to become cool. Gradually the mists receded and she became aware of a white-clad figure moving quietly round the room. She must certainly have been ill to warrant the attention of a nurse! She struggled to speak, but could only manage a faint thread of sound and fell back exhausted on her pillow.

Instantly the nurse was at her side. 'Well, well, so you're conscious! Feeling better?'

'Not much,' Lorna said weakly. 'Can't talk.'

'I'm not surprised. You haven't stopped for the last ten days!'

'Ten?'

'That's right. Nearly eleven, in fact. You were quite a sick young woman. Which reminds me, it's time for your milk. Do you want it mixed with Horlicks or Ovaltine or can you drink it straight?'

Lorna endeavoured a smile. 'Straight.' The nurse moved to the door. 'You speak English well,' Lorna whispered after her.

The woman turned and grinned. 'I should do. I was born in Manchester! Senhor Rodriguez thought you'd prefer to have one of your own countrywomen look after

T—D

you while you were ill. Now, no more talking. Have a
little doze while I get you your drink.'

Obediently Lorna closed her eyes, but her brain was
too active for her to sleep. Why had Rafael gone to so
much trouble to get her an English nurse? After all that
had transpired between them she would have expected
him to wash his hands of her completely – yet he had
done exactly the opposite! She sighed and turned her
head into the pillow. Impossible to try and puzzle out the
complexities of Rafael's nature.

It was the end of the week before she was allowed out
of bed and propped up in an armchair by the window.
Amalia was her first visitor and Lorna was delighted to
see her. 'It seems as if I've been in bed a year. A fine one
I am – the very time when you need me most I have to
get sunstroke!'

'Never mind.' Gingerly Amalia seated herself on the
edge of the bed. 'All's well that ends well. You gave us
quite a shock, though. You were terribly ill the first two
days.'

It was some time before Lorna recovered her strength.
She would never have believed that sunstroke could be
so enervating and she could hardly summon enough
energy to walk about her room. After another week she
was able to dress herself and have her first meal downstairs.

Everyone was in the dining-room to greet her. Manoel
and Rafael had come home from Lisbon for the occasion,
and Lorna felt absurdly shy as she walked in. She was
looking anything but her best. Her hair was lustreless and
tied back from her face with a narrow ribbon, her tan had
waned and her cheekbones protruded sharply, throwing
blue shadows under her eyes. All in all, she thought, a
most unprepossessing picture!

The Senhora smiled a welcome from the head of
the table. 'It's good to have you with us again, Miss
Fairfax.'

With a murmured 'Thank you,' Lorna slipped into a seat beside Rosalia. She was intensely conscious of Rafael's scrutiny, and stubbornly avoided his eyes, concentrating determinedly on the girl by her side.

The meal was a pleasant one. Manoel and Amalia bickered lightly, but no one took any notice; Rosalia attacked her food as if trying to make up for lost time and the Senhora presided graciously over everyone's needs. Only Rafael was the same: cool, polite and heartbreakingly distant.

'You have not eaten much, Miss Fairfax.' It was the Senhora again, her bird-like glance going from Lorna's face to her plate. 'But perhaps it is to be expected. Even now you look far from well. I was saying earlier to Amalia that it might be better if you returned home. A more invigorating climate – your family—'

'Miss Fairfax has no family.' For the first time Rafael spoke.

'She has an aunt,' his mother corrected. 'Apart from which, when one is ill one does not want to be among strangers.'

'After all this time Miss Fairfax should know us better than to regard us as strangers.' He looked at Lorna. 'Am I not right?'

She hesitated. 'I'm very happy here, of course, but I know what your mother means. You may be right, senhora. Perhaps it would be best if I leave.'

'You can't leave now.' Amalia put down her knife and fork. 'You promised, Lorna!'

'Amalia!' Manoel pleaded. 'Don't get excited.'

'I'm not excited!' his wife cried. 'Can't I say anything without being—'

'That's enough!' Rafael was master of the situation. 'There's no need for argument. Miss Fairfax will remain here. She became ill while in our home and it is only right for her to recover fully before she leaves. Now, Miss

Fairfax, I suggest a drive in the country after lunch. I have to go to Cintra on business and a change of air will do you good.'

Lorna swallowed hard. 'I – it – it sounds very nice, but I—?'

'Good. It's settled.' He pushed back his chair. 'Perhaps we can have coffee immediately, Mother. I would like to leave right away.'

With heightened colour the Senhora rang the bell and the meal was finished in awkward silence.

Lorna viewed the afternoon ahead of her with something like despair. Desire to be with Rafael fought with fear that she would not be able to bear his proximity. She had no resistance with which to defend herself from his taunts, one jibe and she knew she would dissolve into tears. Desperately she hoped that Luiz would drive them, but when she went down to the car, Rafael was already at the wheel. The thought of being alone with him all the afternoon was too much for her and she caught at the car door.

'I didn't want to argue with you in front of your family, senhor, but I – don't want to go with you this afternoon. We can have nothing to say to each other and it is stupid to try and pretend to a – a regard that both of us know is false.'

'I know nothing of the kind.' His voice was completely unemotional and he caught her arm and pulled her gently into the car. Unable to argue any longer, she sat in the far corner, her hands trembling so violently that she hid them in the folds of her dress.

'There is no need to be afraid, Lorna,' he said quietly. 'Although we always seem to quarrel when we are alone together, this afternoon will be one occasion when we won't. Now don't answer me. Lean your head back against the seat and rest.'

Exhausted from the effort of trying to defy him, Lorna did as she was told and the miles sped by without a word.

Idly she watched the countryside flash past: scraggy trees and undulating fields ready for harvesting.

The town of Cintra was ten miles distant and stood at the base of an immense, rocky crag. A few houses sprawled up the hill, half hidden by elms, walnuts and the rich green of lemon trees. The dusty square was bounded on one side by the Royal Palace – now a museum – and on the other by the Central Hotel, while high above them, against the blue sky, could be glimpsed the magnificent turrets of Pena Palace.

Rafael parked the car and guided her across the square to the small terrace of the Hotel Central. It was full of people, mostly American tourists, and the hot, sultry air was broken by cries of 'Hey, take a look at this', and 'Move outa the way, Mom, I wanna take a movie!'

Lorna caught Rafael's eye and smiled. 'It's strange how a language mirrors the character of its people.'

'Personally I prefer the lilting beauty of French or the passion of Spanish or Portuguese. Even the cold precision of English is better than that rough camaraderie.' He ordered tea from the waitress and then turned back to her. 'When I think of the different races that inhabit the earth I'm not surprised there are wars.'

'But what's the solution – or isn't there one?'

'There's a solution for everything. It sometimes takes a little while to find one, that's all.' He waved an arm. 'If only the common peoples would intermingle. Then you would find your hope for the future.'

She steeled herself to look directly at the dark, tanned face, the thin mouth now relaxed and gentle. In white flannels and shirt he looked alien to the vociferous young men around him in their gaily coloured shirts and wide-brimmed hats.

'I can just see you giving up your nationality and mingling! You're so proud of being Portuguese you wouldn't want to lose one of your characteristics!'

'Not lose them,' he said, 'but subdue them so that they do not grate on other people.'

'They. don't!' The words were out before she could stop them, and she flushed.

'Yet my ardour grated on you,' he said softly. 'You were more used to phlegmatic men like Simmons.'

She put her hands under the table to hide their trembling. 'I was speaking generally. It isn't fair to be personal.'

'I can never be otherwise with you.' He leaned forward and caught her arm. 'Why is it that whenever I want to say anything to you there are so many people around? I am not a patient man, Lorna, I cannot sit here and look at you without letting you see in my eyes exactly what I feel. *Querida, querida,* we've wasted so much time, there's been so much misunderstanding.'

'It wasn't my fault, Rafael, I knew I was wrong and I apologized.'

'I'm not concerned with the ring,' he said impatiently. 'That's over and done with.'

'I can't forget it,' she said quietly, amazed that he could dismiss so lightly something that had given her infinite pain. 'You were cruel, Rafael, cruel and hurtful.'

'Because I loved you. You know that, you're not blind.'

She stared at him incredulously, unable to believe he had spoken words she had never thought to hear from him. The noise of the people around seemed to diminish; the brilliant light grew dark and then returned with such force that she clung to the edge of the table, her face waxy pale.

Instantly Rafael was on his feet, his arm around her waist. 'What a fool I am! Your first day out and I upset you. My poor darling.' Murmuring softly in Portuguese, he half led, half carried her to the car and settled her in the seat, then slid in beside her and headed towards Estoril.

Gradually Lorna recovered her equilibrium and with it the memory of everything Rafael had said. She gave an

incoherent murmur and he looked at her, his hands tightening on the wheel as he saw the expression in her half-
closed eyes. Without a word he turned the car on to a
narrow rutted lane, drew it to a stop and pulled her into
his arms. Gently and tenderly his lips sought hers, his
kiss telling her more clearly than words of his desire to
protect and cherish rather than to take. For a long time
there was silence, then he drew back from her and lit a
cigarette.

'It is safer this way,' he murmured. 'You are too lovely,
Lorna. I cannot hold you in my arms and remember you
are still an invalid.'

Afraid to believe what her senses told her, she looked
down at the handkerchief in her hands and twisted it
into a crumpled ball. 'What are you trying to tell me,
Rafael? Forgive me if I'm stupid, but—'

'You are not stupid, my darling. I am telling you that
I love you deeply and that I would give the whole world
to make you happy.' He leaned over and tilted her chin
up, forcing her to look into his eyes. 'Surely you are not
surprised at what I am saying. Where is this wonderful
feminine intuition of yours? You must know I loved you
from the moment I saw you sitting in the shadow of the
pavilion with a crayon in your hand.'

She caught her breath. 'I didn't then – not then. But
afterwards, a long time afterwards – I felt . . . I hoped . . .
But you were so cruel, so unforgiving, I couldn't believe
you loved me.'

His sleek head bent to hers. 'If I hadn't I would have
forgiven you more easily: it was because I loved you that
I judged you so harshly. I made the mistake of thinking
you were as strong as I.'

'I'm not, Rafael. I never pretended to be.'

'I know. That was my mistake, I forgot that you were
not like the women I have known all my life. Their
loyalty is emotional, but yours must be mental, too. You
listen to your head as well as your heart.'

'I tried to listen to my heart, Rafael.'

'I know you did, darling.' He moved to take her in his arms, but drew back. 'No, if I hold you I cannot think properly, and there is so much I want to say. I'm not an easy man to love, Lorna, I've never learnt the lesson of humility and deserve all the things you said to me. I'm autocratic and domineering, proud and demanding, but whatever I ask of you I'd give you back tenfold. All I want is for you to love me a little.'

Lorna's voice was thick with unshed tears. 'Not a little, my darling, but so much that I'll never be able to tell you.'

Without another word they were in each other's arms.

At last he put her away from him. 'You are tired, my love. It is time I took you home. I am glad everything is settled, though, now I can turn my mind to business. Another month of such indecision and I would have been bankrupt. I could think of nothing but you!'

'I hope you won't forget me now. I've said yes.' She broke off and a red tide of colour stained her cheeks. Awkwardly she tried to bridge the silence, but he stopped her muffled words with his hand.

'Did I forget the most important thing of all, my dearest? Of course you will be my wife. You didn't think I was suggesting a mésalliance?' He watched the colour sweep into her cheeks again and laughed softly. 'I shall enjoy teaching you the meaning of the word love, my dear one. If only the next few weeks would fly away! I would like us to be married immediately. We have waited long enough.'

She shook her head uncomprehendingly. 'You must give me time to get used to the idea, Rafael. I can't take it all in.'

'You will get used to the idea more quickly when we are married! I love you, Lorna,' he said passionately. 'Every day and night we're apart is a wasted one.'

She laughed softly. 'I think that's what I love about

you most, Rafael — your belief that everyone's going to agree with you. I don't think I'd have the heart to oppose you even if I wanted to!' She rested her head against his shoulder and felt him tremble at her touch. 'You must tell your family first, darling. I don't think your mother will be pleased at the news.'

'Why not?'

'Because she'd prefer you to marry a Portuguese.

'Well, I don't choose to, and no one can dictate to me.'

'Darling, be sensible.'

He caught her hand and kissed it. 'How can I be sensible when you call me 'darling' in that cold little way of yours?'

'I'm not cold,' she protested.

He made a movement as if he were going to test out her statement, but she shook her head.

'No, Rafael, let me speak first! You may think I'm being fanciful about your mother, but I can't help it. I know she'll disapprove of our marriage and I couldn't bear any arguments now. You've got to give me a little time to get stronger — to feel more like myself.' She gave a small, bitter laugh. 'I'm beginning to know how Rosalia felt that night in the pavilion.'

He was shocked into anger. 'How can you say such a thing? You are mad! Why should my mother's disapproval mean so much to you? We are the two people concerned. No one else's opinion should make any difference to us.'

'I know I'm being childish,' she pleaded, 'but can't you understand what I'm trying to say? Let's keep our engagement secret for a little while and give your mother a chance to get used to the idea that you — you like me.'

'She would have to be blind not to know I adore you! How can I hide my feelings for you, Lorna? I'm not made of stone.'

'But a few weeks...'

Reflectively he rubbed his hand across his chin. 'Very well. For a few weeks. But no longer. I am proud that you are going to be my wife and I want all the world to know it.'

CHAPTER SEVEN

'FORTUNE favours the daring' – during the next few days Lorna remembered the Rodriguez motto and wished with all her heart that it was part of her own heritage. There was so much she did not know about Rafael, so much that was strange. Their only bond was their love, and she doubted whether it would be strong enough to surmount the barriers of tradition, race and background.

She had asked Rafael to keep their engagement secret because of his mother, yet her reason went deeper than that. She would have to become accustomed to the idea of turning her back on England, to forsake her mother tongue for a foreign language and accept a new way of life as her own. Would she be able to maintain her own personality amongst all these strangers – to stop herself being absorbed into a way of life with which she did not wholly agree?

And then there was the question of fidelity. Surely Rafael must know she would never allow her marriage to become a replica of Manoel and Amalia's? The more she thought about it the more confused he became. There were so many difficulties they had not acknowledged, so many rocks lying beneath the surface that could wreck their life together.

But with that arrogance that was an essential part of him, Rafael refused to admit that there was anything they could not overcome.

'You are enlarging it out of all proportion,' he said finally. 'It is merely a matter of compromise.'

'Compromise,' she cried in her heart, 'but on whose side?'

If the Senhora noticed a difference in her son's attitude to his cousin's companion she gave no sign of it, and was as studiously polite to Lorna as ever. Since Rosalia's arrival she had begun to take more interest in the house, and Lorna would see her making a tour of inspection, peering into corners, running her fingers along the ledges and occasionally rebuking a maid with an asperity that dissolved the girl to tears.

Amalia was the first to guess the change in Lorna's relationship to Rafael, and one morning as they were strolling in the grounds she taxed her with it.

'You needn't deny it,' she concluded. 'You're positively alight whenever he's round. What's all the secrecy for?'

Lorna paused to pick a flower, holding it in her hands and studying the blossom as intently as if she were Proust. 'I don't think we know each other well enough,' she said at last. 'Why, even in the short time I've been here we've quarrelled like a cat and dog!'

'And you'll go on quarrelling as long as you're not married! I've been through it too. I don't know who said an engagement is the happiest time of your life. You're on edge and ready to fight with your shadow.' She spoke with some of her old animation. 'But heavens, it's perfectly obvious why! Two people in love can't be expected to behave normally when all they want to do is to rush into one another's arms.'

Lorna grinned, 'Now you're being basic!'

'Naturally – it's a basic urge! And you won't solve anything by hesitating.' She looked at her friend curiously. 'You're really *afraid* of Rafael, aren't you?'

'Not in the way you mean.' Lorna pulled the petals of the flower apart until they scattered at her feet like confetti. 'I'm only afraid that he can hurt me as a person. It's difficult to explain . . .

'I know what you mean,' Amalia said soberly. 'I can't say I felt the same with Manoel, but then he and Rafael are like chalk and cheese. No one could ever be afraid of my husband!' She touched Lorna's arm. 'I wish I could help you, but it's something you'll have to overcome yourself. Only don't forget you might hurt Rafael just as easily.'

'I doubt it. He's too strong.'

'And all the more vulnerable. He expects so much from people that he's twice as disillusioned when they let him down. Not that you would,' she said quickly, 'but I'm trying to make you see it from his point of view.'

'I do. That's the trouble,' Lorna sighed. 'And then there's the family. How do you think his mother is going to take it when she hears?'

'She'll probably hate it like hell. But then most mothers do!'

'She wouldn't hate it if it were Inez.'

'Not at first, perhaps, but I doubt if she'd like her for a daughter-in-law once she'd had a sample! I think you're worrying unduly. You'll be surprised how quickly everything will sort itself out once you're married.'

They moved further along the lane and Amalia began to talk of names for her unborn child. In a few moments the conversation was forgotten, yet it lingered disturbingly in Lorna's mind.

As she had expected, Rafael was an impatient lover and the hours they spent together were too infrequent to please him. He disliked having to sit quietly beside her at the dining-room table when he longed to catch her hand in his, or to retire to the opposite end of the room when his body yearned for her nearness.

For her part Lorna disliked the subterfuge even more, and she hated it when he was attentive to Inez, filled with jealousy to see the dark head bent low over the smooth white hand or the black eyes smiling intimately into the amber ones. It was then that she longed to proclaim that he was hers; then too she realized this jealousy would be an integral part of their life together. Rafael would always find women attractive, always be ready with a compliment or a pretty speech. He had all the chivalry of the Latins in his blood and to expect him to be otherwise would be useless.

On one occasion she taxed him with this and he looked at her in amazement.

'Don't you like it when I tell you your hair is like imprisoned sunlight and your eyes are the stars in my dreams?'

'Of course I do. Only I wonder how many times you've said it before.'

'My darling Lorna,' he said dryly, 'the times I said it before are unimportant. It's the times I say it afterwards that count!'

'Well, how many times would you?' she persisted. 'Say it afterwards, I mean.'

'That depends how many women I meet whose hair is like sunlight and whose eyes are stars!'

For a moment Lorna was incredulous, then looking up she saw the twinkle in his eyes.

'You beast, Rafael, you're teasing me!'

'Of course. You didn't expect me to take this nonsense seriously?'

They were sitting in the garden, shaded from the house by trees, and he pulled her on to his lap. 'I think my little English flower is jealous!'

'I am.' Lorna spoke vehemently. 'And I *hate* it. I've fought against it, but it's no good.'

'Of course it's no good,' he said softly. 'Jealousy is a part of love. I'm jealous that these fingers should touch anything but me, jealous of every thought in your head that is not wholly mine. Lorna darling, I can't stand being apart from you much longer. This ridiculous secrecy must end.'

'It will,' she evaded, and stifled his question with her lips. So many times before he had used their passion to subdue her arguments; this time it was her prerogative.

Under the pretext of showing her Portugal, she and Rafael spent long days together, but they came back more conscious of each other than of the beauties they had seen. Through Rafael's eyes the countryside took on a greater meaning, and although she still found it a land of harsh contrasts, of immense riches and degrading poverty, she gradually became accustomed to the differences and grew to understand the economic problems that lay at their root.

On one occasion they spent the evening in the little town of Cacilas, crossing by ferry boat from Lisbon. They dined at the Floresta restaurant, sitting on a balcony, their table overlooking the capital as it climbed its nine hills. One by one the lights came on in the city and the night was crowded with stars. The wide river darkened and the lamps on the boats flickered like fireflies in the mimosa-scented air.

'It's all so beautiful and so different from home,' Lorna sighed.

'Every country is different, my darling, but you'll get to love this one as your own.'

'I hope so, Rafael. You're certainly doing your best to make me.'

'It is not my intention to "make" you do anything, Lorna. You must love Portugal because you want to.'

'It's difficult. It's beautiful, I grant you, but it's still foreign.'

He shot her a keen glance. 'Am I foreign too?'

'Sometimes.'

'And sometimes you're foreign to me.' Her eyes widened and he nodded.

'That surprises you, doesn't it? But it shouldn't. There are many things you say and do that I cannot understand. When you laugh and I don't know what you're laughing about, when your cool eyes rest on me as they do now and I wonder what you are thinking, how you are judging me.'

'I never judge you.'

'My darling, you always judge the person you love.'

'Then how do you judge me?'

'As a tightly closed flower that will, I hope, unfold its petals to the Portuguese sun.'

His lips were almost touching her ear, his breath warm on the nape of her neck, yet no one took any notice. Occasionally dark eyes glanced at the swarthy-skinned, handsome Portuguese and the silver-haired English girl but then moved away again. They are lovers, the looks seemed to suggest, leave them to their pleasure!

The days passed in an even tenure of happiness, each one like a jewel that reflected their love in dazzling colours. But one evening as they sat in the drawing-room listening to music the Senhora broke through the final haunting cadenza as it echoed across the large room.

'Inez was telling me she intends to return home the day after tomorrow, Rafael. I think it would be a good idea if we all went out to dinner for her last evening.'

'Nothing would please me more, Mamma, but I have already made arrangements.' He smiled at Inez. 'I had no idea you were going back so soon. You have only been here a week.'

'I had a letter from my mother today saying she is not well,' Inez moved her head so that the lamplight reflected on the smooth chignon on the nape of her neck. 'I don't live far away, Rafael. Why not come and see us? Papa loves to have you.'

'At the moment it is difficult, but I will write to your father when I have a weekend free.'

'Are you sure you can't manage to come back with me tomorrow?'

'I am going to Alcobaco with Lorna. It was arranged some days ago.'

Inez caught her full lower lip between pointed teeth and when she spoke it was with deceptive sweetness. 'It is not good for Miss Fairfax's reputation that you are alone so much.'

'Lorna would consider that remark old-fashioned,'

Rafael said curtly. 'She thinks our ideas of chaperoning completely out of date, don't you, my dear?'

Forced into the conversation, Lorna had no option but to reply. 'I'm afraid I do, rather, but that's only because I'm used to being independent.'

Inez smoothed her hair. 'Here, we consider it part of the thrill of the chase for a man to know he cannot be alone with a woman.'

'Then I'm glad I'm not Portuguese. I'd find it degrading to be watched all the time as if I couldn't be trusted.'

'It is not a question of trust, merely—'

'There's little point in arguing, Inez.' The Senhora came into the fray. 'Your ideas and Miss Fairfax's are so different there can be no common meeting ground. I am sure she will have much with which to amuse her friends when she returns home.'

'Please don't think I'm ridiculing your ideas,' Lorna protested. 'It's only that I don't see why everyone should find a man and woman guilty because they're alone together. It speaks of – of – nastiness always to jump to dishonourable conclusions.'

There was an awkward silence and Lorna was intensely aware of Rafael pulling at his lip, his brow set mutinously. But she was unprepared for his next action, for he stood up, switched off the radiogram, slammed down the lid and turned to face them.

'It is time we told them the truth, Lorna! I am tired of these petty arguments and jealousies.' He looked directly at his mother. 'You must realize that Lorna was brought up differently from the women here. We consider her ways strange and she is entitled to think the same way about us. But—' he moved over to Lorna and placed an arm around her shoulders, his muscles tense and hard – 'But I will have no criticism of my fiancée. Lorna has consented to be my wife and we intend to get married as soon as possible.'

In the startled silence that followed Lorna's eyes

travelled from face to face: Inez venomous, Amalia radiant, and Manoel and Rosalia registering nothing but complete astonishment, while behind them all the Senhora's black-clad figure was shrunken and with-drawn. Then as if a camera clicked, action began again.

Amalia clapped her hands. 'What wonderful news! I've been waiting for it all along.' She hurried over to Lorna and kissed her. 'I'm terribly happy for you, and you too, Rafael!'

Rafael smiled without taking his eyes from his mother.

'Well, Mama, I am waiting for you to say something.'

'There is nothing for me to say. You know how I feel.' The old lady's voice was harsh. 'I congratulate Miss Fair-fax on captivating you.'

Lorna felt Rafael's arm tighten, but he spoke smoothly. 'You must call her Lorna now, Mama.'

'Of course, I was forgetting. I have been so used to thinking of her as Miss Fairfax ... Forgive me – er – Lorna, I did not mean to be rude.'

'I'm sorry it was such a surprise to you, senhora,' Lorna said quickly. 'Rafael wanted to tell you earlier, but I – I – was afraid.'

'Indeed?' The glance was rapier-sharp. 'What was there for you to be afraid of?'

'Lorna was not afraid for herself,' Rafael interposed quickly. 'She only thought it might be – er – unexpected for you.'

'It is always unexpected when one's son chooses a wife.'

For an instant the old lady's eyes flickered towards Inez, and as if recognizing the unspoken order Rafael walked over to the girl.

'And you, Inez? Will you congratulate me?'

'Naturally. I think Miss Fairfax is an extremely lucky woman.'

'Why is everyone congratulating Lorna?' Rosalia spoke for the first time. 'Personally I think Rafael's the lucky one! I wouldn't like to be married to him! He's so obstinate – you don't know what you're letting yourself in for, Lorna. I wouldn't marry him for all the sardines in Oporto!'

The tension eased and it seemed to Lorna that the family pattern, like a kaleidoscope when shaken, subtly changed. At the centre of the new design was the warm red glow of their love, shading into the subtle pinks of Amalia's delight but broken by the green of the Senhora's jealousy and the black of Inez's hate.

Now that their engagement was formally announced there was no need to resort to subterfuge in order to meet, and Lorna suggested to Rafael that they cancel the following day's excursion.

'I'm sure you've been neglecting your work lately, darling, and I'll be perfectly all right on my own. In any case, Amalia hasn't seen me for so long I'm beginning to feel guilty.'

'You should only feel guilty when you are not looking after me! Amalia has enough people at her beck and call.'

'But if it hadn't been for her we'd never have met.'

'Do you really believe that, my darling?' He came close, so close that she could feel the warmth emanating from him. 'Do you think I wouldn't have found you wherever you'd been hiding? Don't you know it was written in the stars the moment we were born? You are the blossom on my tree, the grass growing out of my earth.'

Listening to his deep voice murmur words of love Lorna felt her calm logic disintegrate. Unthinkable to imagine herself married to another man, to surrender her lips, her body, to anyone except this tall, dark Portuguese.

Rafael came down to earth first. 'I'm afraid you're right about my neglecting my work. This excursion will have to be the last for some time. There's a mountain of work to get through before we can take that long honeymoon I dream about.'

'Do you want a long honeymoon?' she asked demurely.

'All our life will be a honeymoon, my love.' Gently he bit the lobe of her ear. 'Remember that and nothing can go wrong.'

At the end of the week Rafael went to Oporto on business, and although dismayed at his departure Lorna was able to relax for the first time since their engagement. She had still not fully recovered from her attack of sunstroke, and his ardent lovemaking of the past week seeemed to have drained her of all vitality. His presence in a room set her body trembling and she was shaken by such longing for him that she could not believe herself to be the same carefree, light-hearted girl who had left England such a short time ago. Being engaged was certainly a strain, she thought half-humorously, and she could almost agree with Amalia that it was not quite the idyllic time it appeared to be. Remembering her friend, Lorna's satisfaction disappeared, and with a feeling of guilt she hurried downstairs to find her.

Amalia was lying on the couch in the drawing-room. She had altered considerably in the last few weeks and spent most of her time dreaming of cool winds and the pleasure of being slim again.

'Do you know, Lorna, I haven't seen my feet for ages, except in a mirror!'

'Never mind. It'll soon be over, and then think of the relief.'

'Rather like a lunatic who bangs his head on a brick wall for the pleasure of stopping!'

'You won't feel like that when you hold your baby in your arms. And you'll take the second and third in your stride!'

'Heaven forbid! One is quite enough.'

Lorna shook her head. 'It's horrible to be an only child.'

I was, and it never bothered me. Although perhaps that was because I lived with my mother's family and there were about eighteen cousins under one roof!'

'The only time you'd get so many relations together in England would be at Christmas!' Lorna grimaced. 'I'd go mad if I had to put up with the family all the year round.'

'You'll have to change your views when you marry. You don't think the Senhora's going to pack up, do you? This is her house, and she'll stay here till she dies.'

Lorna stared. 'I never thought of that. I took it for granted she'd move out when Rafael and I married.'

'Well, she won't, and Rafael won't ask her to either. Why, he'd be horrified at the idea.'

Too well Lorna knew Amalia was speaking the truth. In the short time of her engagement she had learned enough of Rafael to know he would brook no opposition from his wife when it came to any family matter.

'But surely he knows his mother isn't pleased at our engagement?' she said at last. 'I'd think he'd want her out of the house for that reason alone.'

'He's probably hoping that once you're his wife she'll climb down. Anyway, there won't be much she can do.'

Lorna let this pass. 'And what about Rosalia? Will she be here, too?'

'Naturally. This is her home until she marries again.'

'Lord! I can't see Rafael and me having a life of our own for the next ten years!'

'If you were thinking of dinner à deux you can think again! Rosalia's sweet, but she hasn't much tact, and the Senhora'll be watching you like a hawk. She's not bad as an aunt, but I can't say I'd fancy her as a mother-in-law.' She yawned. 'Still, I wouldn't worry too much about it. You'll have Rafael on your side for the first few years at least, and if you want to make any drastic changes do them in the first flush of love, if you wait too long you've had it.' She shifted her position again. 'Be a dear and pass me the stool, I'll put my feet up for a bit.' Lorna complied, and Amalia stretched her arms above her head and closed her eyes.

The sun beat down mercilessly, but they were shaded by the terrace, the gloom intensified by the brilliant light outside. Lorna was sitting in the hammock, her legs curled beneath her. In a white cotton sun-dress, her shoulders bare, her hair swinging loosely, she looked younger and infinitely prettier than when she had arrived in Portugal.

'When are you going to buy your trousseau, Lorna?' Amalia opened her eyes. 'And your wedding dress – will it be white?'

'I haven't thought about it. I'll have to go home to buy my things anyway – I've got no money here.'

'Rafael will give you what you need. If I know him he's already made up his mind what he wants you to wear!'

'That's one thing he won't get away with. The wedding dress is *my* secret.'

'Will your aunt come over for the wedding?'

'I hope so.'

'Then there's no point in your going back. You might as well take the money from Rafael.'

Lorna's chin lifted. 'He might pay for my things in future, but I've no intention of allowing him to do so yet.'

'What won't you allow?'

They both turned in surprise as Senhora Rodriguez walked out on to the terrace. In the inevitable black crêpe, tide at the wrist and high at the throat, she made no concession to the heat.

'What won't you allow my son to do?' she reiterated. 'I presume you *were* referring to Rafael.'

Lorna flushed. 'My trousseau and wedding dress – I said I wouldn't let him buy it for me.'

'I see.' The Senhora sat down, placing her black malacca stick with its silver handle against the back of her chair. 'Strange that you should be reluctant to take money from him. I should have thought you would be exactly the opposite.'

Lorna stopped swinging the hammock. 'What do you mean by that?'

'Why, nothing, my dear.'

'I think you did. I'd rather you told me straight out, senhora. It's not like you to be afraid.'

A flush rose in the papery cheeks. 'I am not afraid, Miss – er – Lorna. I was merely surprised that you should show scruples at taking money from my son. To my mind it is one of your prime reasons for marrying him.'

Lorna stood up angrily. To know what Rafael's mother thought was one thing, to hear her say it so crudely was another. 'I think you've gone too far this time, senhora. I've no intention of staying here to be insulted!'

'Then you should go. While we are under the same roof there can be no armistice.'

'I see.' Lorna's breath was a sigh. 'Now we're really coming into the open. You'd like me to go, wouldn't you? It's what you've been hoping for ever since you saw Rafael was falling in love with me. Well, you won't prevent our marriage, however hard you try.'

'I've no intention of trying. I leave that to you.'

'What do you mean?'

'That I've been aware of your indecision for weeks.'

'That's not true! There's been no indecision. But why am I bothering to explain to you? You're determined to believe I'm marrying your son because of his money and you'll twist everything I say. I love Rafael, and whether you believe it or not I'd marry him if he didn't have a penny. I'd prefer it, in fact! You can't understand that, can you? Can't understand that I'd rather he were poor than rich. You've built your life up around your money and you think it can buy you everything you want. Well, it can't! It can't buy you love or affection, nor prevent it, either. You're trying to make me believe you've got Rafael's interest at heart when all you want to do is keep him for yourself. You're a jealous, spiteful old woman and—'

'What if I am? I have a right to be jealous of my son! It was my body that suffered when he was born, my love

that grew with his first words, his first tottering steps. My
life went into the making of him, and I did not bring him
up to marry someone who will destroy him!'

'Why should I destroy him?' Lorna said hotly. 'We
love each other.'

'At the moment. But what of the years to come? How
can your love grow and deepen when there are no roots
to strengthen it? You might think you know what's best
for him, but you don't!' She stood up and reached for
her stick. 'You won't be happy living here, my child. In a
few months, a year, you will make Rafael unsure of everything he has always taken for granted. You might think
you have won, but it will be a bitter victory. Ties of blood
are stronger than anything you can weave around him,
and in the end he will come back here! I might concede
that you love him in your own way, but you will never
understand him – never!' She turned and walked into
the drawing-room, the sound of her stick echoing on the
parquet floor.

Lorna wiped her forehead. It was wet, like her hands.

'I'm sorry you had to listen to all this, Amalia. It must
have been horrible for you.'

'It was worse for you!' Amalia came over and sat next
to Lorna on the hammock. 'I knew my aunt didn't like
you, but I never guessed how much. I wouldn't take what
she said too seriously, though. She was only being spiteful.'

Lorna shuddered and rested against the canvas back.
'If only I could believe that! But she wasn't lying,
Amalia! She believes she was speaking the truth!'

'She's not a prophet.'

'But she knows her son.'

'So do you. And what's more you know yourself and
how you'll act. She was only guessing. I don't see any
reason why you shouldn't be perfectly happy living here
if you want to.'

'If you want to.' The words had a familiar ring. But did

she want to? Lorna sighed and stood up. If only she knew
the real answer to that question her way would be clear.

At dinner that night the Senhora was her usual self and
Lorna had to admire the self-control which enabled her
to sit at the head of the table and act as if nothing had
happened. Manoel was working late in Lisbon and
Amalia went to her room immediately after coffee. One of
the maids had taught her to crochet and she whiled away
the time by making a shawl, the white wool grubby from
being wound and unwound repeatedly.

As soon as she could Lorna stood up. 'If you'll excuse
me, senhora, I'll take a stroll along the promenade.'

'Portuguese women do not go out alone so late,
Lorna.'

'I'm not a Portuguese woman,' Lorna said quietly.

'Even so, you should learn to accept our customs.'

'I'll go with you,' Rosalia interposed. 'If you'll wait a
moment, I'll get my coat.'

Soon the two girls were walking along the dark promenade. The lights were strung intermittently and only the
cafés under the arcades were open, the tables for the most
part deserted. It was late in the season and in another
few weeks the tourists would depart. How would she feel
living in a town where there would be no English-speak-
ing voices? She sighed and looked at Rosalia.

'You seem sad, Lorna.' Rosalia's light voice was
troubled. 'Is anything wrong?'

'I was just wondering how you felt now you're home
again.'

'As if I'd never been away. Sometimes it's even difficult
to remember I was married.' She sighed. 'I'm lucky things
ended the way they did.'

'Do you feel bitter? About your husband, I mean.'

'I try not to. I didn't love him when he died, you know.
I haven't told the others, but I can talk more easily to you.
Perhaps it's because you're both English.'

'I thought he came from Australia.'

'He was born in London, but he worked for an uncle on a sheep farm in New South Wales.'

'What made you marry him?'

'I don't know. Looking back I'd say it was the novelty of meeting someone who didn't treat me as if I were a piece of porcelain.' She smiled wryly. 'I soon realized how much nicer it was *not* to be looked on as an equal! We didn't think the same about anything. He expected me to be able to do all the things the Australian women did, and when he found I couldn't, we quarrelled.'

'But what did they do that you couldn't?'

'Everything. Keep house, shop, cook.'

'There's nothing difficult in that. If you'd wanted to learn . . .'

'Ah, but I didn't. That was the trouble.' Rosalia tightened her scarf and threw Lorna a half smile. 'You mustn't blame me altogether. Don't forget I was brought up to do nothing. I never even turned on the water for my bath!'

'No wonder you quarrelled! Didn't you even try to make an effort in the beginning?'

'Naturally. But everything was twice as hard for me.' She shrugged. 'Environment makes you what you are, Lorna, and you can't fight against it.'

Fingers of doubt stirred in Lorna's mind at this echo of the Senhora's words. It was like a conspiracy – another doubt, another hint. Desperately she tried again.

'But didn't your love for Frank make you try to be what he wanted? What would have happened if he hadn't been killed?'

'I often ask myself that,' Rosalia's gay face sobered. 'It's easy enough to fall in love, but to go on loving when you're both pulling different ways . . . You've got to be a saint to do that.'

'How about Juan? Would you consider him again?'

'With a wife and two children?'

Lorna smiled. 'Sorry, that was a bad guess on my part!

Never mind, though, you're pretty enough to marry again soon.'

'I've no doubt,' Rosalia said dryly. 'Rafael will find someone as soon as he can.'

Lorna stared in bewilderment. 'Wouldn't you like to choose your husband yourself?'

'Why should I? Look at the mess I made before.'

'But even so ... I wouldn't let anyone tell me whom to marry.'

'It's the custom in Portugal.

'Custom! Custom! Must everything be done because it's the custom? No wonder you're a hundred years behind the times!'

'Better not let Rafael hear you say that. He loves his country and he'll expect you to feel the same.' She caught Lorna's arm. 'Look at the view, isn't it wonderful? See how the water shimmers in the moonlight and the little fortress on the cliff. Oh, it's good to be home again!'

They began to retrace their steps, walking towards the station. On their right a low wall separated them from the railway line, on their left loomed the distant bulk of the Casino and the twinkling lights of the Palace hotel. The wide road was deserted except for an occasional car and they seemed to be the only couple abroad.

'Let's go back another way,' Rosalia said as they crossed the road. 'We can walk along the gardens and turn off higher up. It will bring us to the back of the house and we can slip in through the kitchen.'

They set off briskly and Lorna pulled her coat tight around her. Although it had been unbearably hot during the day the usual wind had sprung up the moment the sun had set, and it whipped round them now with true Atlantic force. Breathlessly they climbed until Rosalia stopped.

'*Porra!* I've got a stone in my shoe. I wish they'd do something about these roads.' She hobbled over to a bench and sat down. 'A piece of gravel's worked its way inside my stocking.' Grumbling, she bent to dislodge it, and Lorna walked slowly up the steep path. Twenty yards ahead a black car was parked and as she came abreast she stared into it curiously. With a gasp she drew back into the shadows. Manoel was in the front seat with a woman in his arms! Without thinking she turned and ran down the way she had come.

'Let's go back the other way, Rosalia! It's dark and I'm frightened.'

'Whatever for? Gracious, Lorna, you're as pale as a ghost.'

'I know. I thought I saw someone hiding in the shadows. Please, Rosalia, let's go the other way.'

'Very well, I don't mind.' The Portuguese girl stood up. 'Come on, give me your hand and we'll run.'

Arm in arm they sped down the hill and along the promenade.

It was not until she reached the quiet of her room that Lorna's anger at Manoel returned with a force that left her shaken. What would Rafael say when she told him of this latest development? Surely even he would not condone an illicit love affair, for love affair it undoubtedly was: she knew Manoel too well to believe he would stop at kisses. The more she thought about it the more contemptuous she became, and she could hardly restrain herself until Rafael returned from Oporto and she was able to tell him the news.

He listened with his usual attentiveness and when she had finished stared into the empty fireplace contemplatively before he spoke.

'What do you want me to do?'

'Speak to him, of course. You don't think he can carry on like this without Amalia finding out?'

'But what good will it do if I tell him?'

She was taken aback. 'It will stop him.'

'Will it? Do you really think so? Honestly, Lorna, this is too much! Not only do I have my own worries but I must bother about this stupid cousin of mine.' He swore beneath his breath. 'I'd like to break his damn neck! If he has to have a woman why must he find one here?'

Lorna swung round, livid with anger. '*Has* to? What do you mean *has* to? If he hasn't the decency to be faithful when his wife's expecting a baby —'

'For goodness' sake leave the baby out of it! Why does a woman always use a child to fetter a man?' He stopped at the stricken look on Lorna's face. 'Darling, I'm sorry, I didn't mean it that way.'

He came towards her, but she moved back. 'No, Rafael, don't touch me! I couldn't bear it now.' She looked at him in bewilderment. 'How can you speak so calmly of Manoel having an affair? And he says he loves his wife! What does he know about love? What do you know about love if you can even think of him without disgust?'

'Men are not so easily disgusted, nor do they set so much store by unfaithfulness!' He banged his hand down on the desk. 'Why do you keep tormenting yourself like this? Why do you persist in distorting everything?'

'I don't! But I can't help seeing Manoel and Amalià as a mirror for our future. If you behaved like Manoel it would be the end of everything! I'll never look at another man once I'm your wife, never let anyone come near me or touch me, and I'd expect you to do the same.'

'Why do you think I wouldn't?' he said angrily. 'Why must you make me into something I'm not?'

'I'm not making you into anything! I'm only telling you what I feel.'

Without replying he sat down at his desk and buried his head in his hands. The ormolu clock on the mantelpiece ticked by a minute before he spoke, his voice muffled and indistinct.

'I don't understand you, Lorna. You've beaten me. I can't go on taking your constant distrust and jealousy. I can't go on fighting a stupid ego that forces you to believe I go from one woman to another before finally coming back to you. Either you control yourself now or you'll destroy us both.'

'Rafael, I —' Lorna's throat worked convulsively and she could not go on. Instead she knelt by his side and put her arms around his neck, her tears warm against his cheek. For a moment he resisted, then with a muffled exclamation he pulled her into his arms and held her tight.

'Dearest heart of mine, why must we hurt each other? How many times do I have to tell you that we're different from anyone else? *Cara mia*, don't cry. I promise I'll speak to Manoel.'

'I'm not crying because of Manoel,' she gulped, 'but because of what you just said.'

'I was angry. I did not mean it.' Gently he stroked her hair. 'You should know better than to greet a man with such a long face when he has travelled all the way from Oporto and only wants to hold the woman he loves in his arms.'

'Oh, Rafael, what a stupid beast I am. You must be exhausted.' She showered his face with little kisses. 'How could I have been so selfish?'

He rubbed his cheek against hers. 'If you'll always atone like this I won't mind!'

The following night Rafael took her into Lisbon to dinner. It was quite dark as they drove through the old part of the city, the streets so narrow that it was difficult to manoeuvre the Cadillac round the sharp corners.

He parked the car and escorted her down a dark, mean street, with elegant cars parked on either side. It was surprising to see so much richness amidst poverty, but as they approached the restaurant the flower-decorated vestibule spoke of good food and expensive intimacy. Candles were the only illumination and their flickering picked out the gingham-covered tables and walls decked with photographs of famous personalities.

They were shown to a small table in an alcove facing

a dark dapper pianist and two swarthy guitarists, and Lorna looked around her with interest.

'What an unusual place. Does it specialize in any particular food?'

'Not food, *cara*, music. The *fado* – folk-songs of Portugal. We heard some on the radio.'

'Of course.' She glanced about her. 'Who sings them?'

He indicated a dark-haired woman of about forty who was serving at one of the tables.

'But she's a waitress!'

'She also owns the restaurant! She is not a professional singer, you understand. Indeed, the whole beauty of the *fado* is that it is sung by ordinary men and women.'

'When will she start?'

'As soon as the restaurant is full. It's interesting to watch her: she just throws off her apron and begins to sing.'

'No wonderful introduction or publicity? I can't believe it!'

He beckoned the waiter and ordered the meal without consulting her, an action Lorna found mystifying until the food was brought to the table. It was completely strange to her and she began to eat with curiosity that sharpened to relish as she tasted the concoction of small fish flavoured with spices and decorated with chopped leaves, then a young fowl braised in pimentos and chives followed by whipped cream with wild, sweet raspberries.

They were sipping coffee when a small party of men entered the room and sat down at a table in the far corner. They nodded and waved to Rafael, but made no attempt to come over, and Lorna understood why when three gaudily dressed women came in and joined the party.

'Are they friends of yours?' she enquired.

'Yes.'

'All of them?'

'Only the men.'

She looked behind her curiously. They seemed to be enjoying themselves inordinately and there was loud talk and laughter. She caught the flash of a wedding ring on one man's hand and bit her lip.

'Are they with their wives?'

Aware of the implication underlying her question, Rafael paused in the act of extracting a cigarette from his gold case. 'No. Do you want to continue the subject?'

'There's nothing to say.'

'I agree, but nevertheless there's one thing you should know. The man you are so interested in is a very good friend of mine. He has been married for six years, has four children and a young, wealthy wife who—' he lit his cigarette, 'weighs sixteen stone.'

'I suppose you think that's sufficient explanation.'

'Whether I do or not doesn't matter.' His mouth tightened. 'I refuse to argue with you any more. We've had quite enough discussions for one day.'

As if to further his point the lights dimmed, the pianist played a series of low notes and the proprietress took off her apron and moved to the centre of the room. Then with head thrown back and eyes half closed she began to sing. Her body swayed slowly to the rhythm of the music and her voice had the strange inexpressible longing of the Negro spirituals. Although she sang in the simple manner dictated by tradition she seemed to express all the misery and inarticulate fears of a primitive race. It was like listening to the heartbeat of Portugal itself; a country so steeped in history that it could not shake off the trammels of the past, could not brace itself to acknowledge the realism of the present.

All Lorna's vague disquiet crystallized and for the first time she knew she could never identify herself with this land. The people were in the groove of the sixteenth century: they still irrigated their farms with the shadoof and winnowed the corn by hand, content to eke out an existence as their forefathers had done, or slave all their lives in the shadow of the Quinta. Her thought ended abruptly as the *fado* concluded.

'Did you like it?' Rafael was looking at her curiously.

'It was beautiful.'

'So are you — now more than ever with the lustre of tears in your eyes. Why are you sad?'

Reluctant to spoil the intimacy of their mood, she shook her head. 'Only a woman's fancy. Don't you know we always enjoy a good cry? What was the song about?'

'A peasant left with her child while the husband went to the big city to earn a living. When he returns the baby is dying and there is a grand reconciliation over the death-bed. We like a little melancholy too! One of our poets said the *fado*, the knife and the guitar are the three loves of the Portuguese.'

'I don't mind the first and the last, but you can keep the knife!'

'Oh no. The knife sleeps under the pillow of passion. It is part of our temperament. Aren't you flattered to think I would murder my rival?'

'Certainly not!' she said primly. 'It would be a very un-civilized way to behave!'

His teeth flashed in a smile. 'You don't know how you'd behave in the circumstances, my dearest. Love is like the sea, with the wind of jealousy ready to whip it into angry foam.'

Lorna remembered his words as they drove back along the coast road to Estoril, and she heard the soft lapping of the water on the sand. The night was calm, the velvet sky brilliant with stars, yet the perpetual wind gently moved the branches of the palms and the sand eddied and swirled in delicate spirals.

She was sorry when they drew up in front of the dark house and Rafael opened the door into the hall.

'Wait a minute, Lorna, I've something to show you.'

She followed him into the library and he picked up a green leather box that lay on top of his desk. Without a word he pressed it open and she looked down at a magnificent pearl ring, its smooth sheen reflecting a myriad colours. Rafael lifted it out and slipped it on her finger.

'This is to make our betrothal final.'

'It's beautiful,' she whispered. 'Much too beautiful for me.'

'Nothing is too beautiful for you,' he said, drawing her into his arms. 'Of all my pearls you are the most precious.'

Possessively his lips found hers, compelling her to a passionate response. Misunderstandings of the day disappeared and as if determined to deny their very existence she pressed close against him, her arms caressing the dark hair that grew low on his neck. Their kiss lengthened and deepened, seeming to draw upon her very soul, until with an exclamation he pushed her away.

'You'd better go, Lorna. I won't answer for the consequences if you don't.'

'I don't think I'd care,' she whispered.

For an instant he moved a step towards her, then shook his head. 'No, *querida*, I can't. It wouldn't be fair.' He turned back to the dark. 'Go quickly while I still have the strength to let you.'

CHAPTER EIGHT

INEZ remained a constant visitor to the house, and although Lorna felt no warmth towards her she had to admire the aplomb with which the girl carried off the situation. What a strange race they were, she reflected, violently passionate one moment, yet able to hide their feelings behind a mask of social bonhomie the next. She would never have had the courage to go on seeing Rafael if the position had been reversed, and she suspected that the Senhora was behind the Portuguese girl's continuing presence.

But there were many pleasant interludes; times when the sun shone brightly, the people laughed and the whole world was gay and smiling.

One of the most interesting evenings was the Senhora's dinner party given to introduce her future daughter-in-law to the family. Lorna was amazed at the number of relations, old and young, short and tall, thin and fat, who answered the invitation. Never had she seen seen such a striking family resemblance in so many people, and she thought with amusement that the younger members of the party had only to look at the older members to see how they would look some twenty years hence!

Throughout the evening the Senhora made a great pretence of affection and Lorna wished with all her heart that it was real. She knew without being told that Rafael had quarrelled with his mother over his engagement, and on more than one occasion had interrupted an argument between them, the tightening of the Senhora's lips as she entered the room telling her more clearly than words that she was the cause of the quarrel. Yet Rafael never referred to his mother's attitude, and Lorna felt reluctant to broach the subject, feeling that the first overture must come from him.

As September drew to a close the azure sky became more intensely blue and the sun, sinking lower on the horizon, glowed with an even fiercer heat. The earth was gathered of its harvest and the farmers began to prepare for the stripping of the maize cobs, an event always followed by a party. Lorna had heard a great deal about this ceremony and she was delighted when Rafael promised to take her to one.

'Has it got a special name?' she asked.

'*Esfolhar*. It means to de-leaf.'

'What happens? It seems most mysterious.'

'The only mystery lies in the number of king cobs that are found!' At the puzzlement on her face he smiled. 'I'd better explain from the beginning. The maize cobs are brought into a huge barn and all the young people sit around tearing off the husks and throwing the cobs into a heap which the girls carry out to the *casastra*.'

'What's that – a dance?'

'No, it's just a trough – the dancing comes later. Before that there's the search for the king cob, which is a red one, rare and very much sought after because any man who finds it has the right to kiss all the girls.'

'And if a girl finds it?'

'She may choose a man to kiss.'

'Only one?' Lorna protested. 'That's favouritism!'

'Is it indeed?' He pulled her into his arms and spun her round the room until she begged him to release her. With a final twirl he let her go, but not before he had covered her face with kisses.

'And how many men would you want to kiss?' he asked fiercely.

'That's a leading question.' She shook back her hair. 'Anyway, you should know the answer.'

'I do, but I wanted to hear you say it.' He stooped to

kiss her. 'I must be off, *querida*. Take care of yourself, and
be ready for me when I come home.'

Lorna spent most of the afternoon deciding on a dress
for the *esfolhar*, and finally picked out a circular red
cotton skirt with a white, draw-string blouse. She was
taking it downstairs for one of the maids to iron when she
was called to the phone. It was Rafael, his voice thin and
metallic over the wire.

'Is anything the matter?' she asked breathlessly.

'Nothing to worry about, *cara*. Only that I'm tied up
with some business people and won't get back till late tonight. Perhaps you can get Manoel to take you.'

'I don't want to go without you.'

'Poor darling,' his voice deepened. 'Never mind, there'll
be other *esfolhars*.'

Lorna replaced the receiver with a childish desire to
cry and wandered into the drawing-room where Amalia
was resting.

'You'll strangle yourself with these balls of wool one
day!' She bent to pick up a coloured tangle from the
carpet. 'Rafael's just phoned to say he won't get back in
time for the *esfolhar*.'

'What a pity!' Amalia accepted the wool. 'Still, there'll
be lots more next year and the year after.'

'It won't be the same then.'

'Not if you're my size!' Amalia stretched lazily. 'Gosh,
Lorna, I do feel tired. I've had a pain in my back all day.'

'Would you like me to call the doctor?'

'I don't think so. It'll pass off. It generally does. Thank
goodness I won't have to dress for dinner. Inez and the
Senhora are out, so there'll only be the two of us.'

Lorna straightened a couple of ornaments on the
mantelpiece. 'A pity Senhora Rodriguez hasn't got another son. Then she could have married him off to Inez!'

'She'd never have loved another son like Rafael. It's
funny how some mothers idolize one particular child. I
wonder if I'll be the same?'

'I hope not. There's nothing worse than a parent who's afraid to let go. Do you think she encourages Inez to come here?'

'Why?'

'Because I'd have thought she'd avoid it now Rafael's engaged. I know I would.'

'Inez would think it weak if she stayed away. Anyway, it was only her pride that was hurt. I don't think she was in love with Rafael the way you are. It's my opinion that she comes here now just to annoy you.'

'How petty!'

'Most women are. Especially when they've only got gossip to occupy their minds! That's the trouble over here. Women aren't allowed to do anything useful, and those with a little more intelligence than the rest have to use it up some other way.'

Lorna sat down and began to unravel a pile of wool. 'I suppose it's hard to vegetate when you're a vegetable. I know I can't bear the thought of doing nothing.'

'You'll have to get used to it. By the way, did I tell you we're definitely going back to Brazil at the end of the year?'

Lorna's hands dropped to her lap. 'How wonderful! I'm so glad.'

'So am I. It's what I've been longing for. I feel in my bones that everything will be all right once Manoel and I are out of Portugal. He's not the sort of man to be left alone for long. He's too weak and susceptible to a pretty face.'

There was a short silence, and Lorna looked at Amalia's cumbersome body in its voluminous housecoat, the dark hair limp and drawn back in a simple roll.

'Don't you mind knowing that Manoel's weak?' she said quietly.

'What good would it do me if I did? If there's one thing I've learnt in the past year it's to accept the inevitable. I married Manoel, faults and all, and it would be stupid

of me to try and change him. Not that I intend to sit back
and let him flirt whenever he feels like it – only that I'm
not going to let it break up our marriage.'

'I can't believe it's you talking. That you can be so calm
and – and—'

'Not calm, darling – practical. You might be a few years
older than me, but you're years younger as far as men are
concerned!'

'You talk as if you'd had a lifetime of experience.'

'Married to Manoel I have!'

'Then why did you marry him if you knew all his
faults?'

'Love, I suppose, and the fact that reputation made
him all the more attractive. Doesn't it give you a certain
sense of satisfaction to know that out of all the women he's
known Rafael's chosen you?'

'No, it doesn't!' With a visible effort Lorna relaxed. 'I
keep thinking of all the other women who went before me
and wonder whether there'll be any more after me.'

'What a morbid thing to say! Why, Rafael's crazy
about you! For a bride-to-be you certainly look on the
black side.'

'I know, but I can't help myself. I'd prefer not to get
married at all than be starry-eyed for a year and disillusioned afterwards.'

'Well, there's no guarantee about anything, least of
all marriage. The trouble with you is that you look too
deeply into things. It's not always good to know too much.
When I first—' Her breath caught on a strangled note
and the colour drained from her face.

'Amalia! Lorna rushed over. 'What's the matter —
are you ill?'

'A pain in my side.' The girl straightened up. 'It's gone
now, thank goodness. It might be better if I go and lie
down for a while.'

'Are you sure you wouldn't like to see the doctor?'

'Positive, thanks.'

'Shall I come upstairs with you?'

'I don't think so. I'll be all right on my own. Really, Lorna, it's nothing.'

Amalia walked slowly out of the room and Lorna sat down again on the sofa.

How quiet and peaceful it was here – too peaceful sometimes. She stood up and moved idly round the room wishing there was something she could do. But there was nothing. The house was spotless, the meals delicious and the servants competent and thorough. Why, she had never even gone as far as the kitchens! Ridiculous to think she was going to be mistress of this house and did not know the whereabouts of one of its main rooms. Mistress in name only. Unbidden the words came into her mind and refused to be ousted. Would she and the Senhora always vie for pride of place, with Rafael neutral in the background? Aimlessly she wandered round the downstairs rooms : into the library where the books were all in Portuguese, to the dining-room – laid only for two – and back to the drawing-room with its trailing plants and polished floors. She looked down at the knitting wools on the sofa. What a good thing Amalia would soon be returning to Brazil. How strange Rafael had not told her of this decision, or did he still object to discussing family matters with her?

She sighed and walked upstairs to change for dinner. Ruefully she replaced the skirt and frilly blouse and slipped on a simple cotton dress before she walked down the corridor to Amalia's room.

'You're quick, Lorna. What time is it?'

'After eight. Will you come down for supper or have it sent up?'

'I couldn't eat anything, thanks. But you go on down.'

Lorna was at the door when Amalia called her name. The Portuguese girl was half sitting, half lying on the bed, her eyes dilated with fear.

'I think the pains have begun, Lorna. I – I – feel quite sick – quite odd. Oh, Lorna, what shall I do?'

'Call the doctor, of course! There's no need to be afraid, darling, it's perfectly natural. Give me the doctor's number and I'll telephone him.'

'It's on the pad on the bedside-table.' Amalia's hands clenched and unclenched on the coverlet and she began to cry. 'I wish Manoel were here. I want to see him. I don't know why he isn't back, he promised to be home early.'

'He'll be here soon, darling. Please don't cry. I'll call the doctor.'

'I still want Manoel. It's his place to be with me.' She began to cry even harder, her body shaken with sobs that occasionally ended in a moan of pain.

Trembling, Lorna dialled the doctor's house, the palms of her hands growing damp as she tried to explain what was happening in stumbling Portuguese. The woman at the other end seemed unable to understand and there was silence on the wire. Lorna held on, hoping desperately that she had managed to convey the urgency she felt and breathing a sigh of relief as a man's voice suddenly questioned her in broken English. Briefly Lorna explained again, replacing the receiver with the fervent hope that her message would be relayed.

For the next hour Lorna stood by Amalia's bedside, talking and joking in an effort to distract her. At ten o'clock the doctor arrived and she went out into the corridor to wait for him. It seemed an eternity before he followed her out, and one look at his face told her something was the matter.

'I would like to take my patient to the hospital,' he said quietly.

'Is anything wrong?'

'There are sometimes complications with a first baby. I would feel easier in my mind if the Senhora were in more – more clinical surroundings.'

'Senhor Rodriguez wanted the child to be born here.'

The doctor stroked his small, pointed beard and looked back into the room. 'I know how it is with families. There is a tradition about where the child should be born — especially a Rodriguez! But with this one I am afraid — you understand?'

'Perfectly. You had better make your arrangements.'

'Thank you. I will do so immediately. Do you know where to find the Senhora's husband?'

'I'm not sure. He's out at the moment, but I may be able to get in touch with him.'

'Good. It would be better if he is here.'

He turned back into the bedroom, and Lorna snatched up a light coat and ran down the stairs.

She arrived at the brightly lit portal of the Casino breathless and dishevelled, to find her way barred by a commissionaire.

'Your ticket, please.'

'I haven't got one. I don't want to play. I'm only looking for someone.'

'You cannot go in without a ticket. It is the rule.'

'But I don't want to play, I tell you!'

He shook his head. 'I can let you have a temporary ticket if you like. It is not expensive.'

She felt in her pocket. 'I haven't any money!'

The man said nothing and Lorna looked round desperately, wondering if she could rush past him.

As if guessing her intention he blocked the doorway. 'Why go in if you do not intend to play?'

'I want to find someone. It's terribly important. Can't you let me in for a minute?'

'It's against the rules, senhorita. Who is it?'

'Senhor Rodriguez, but I —'

'Why did you not say so in the first place? The Senhor is well known here.' He held open the door courteously. 'You will find him in the restaurant watching the cabaret.'

With a tight-lipped smile Lorna sped across the marble floor. From the gaming rooms at the side came the click, click of the balls and the subdued murmur of voices occasionally punctuated by the firmer tone of the croupier: 'Vingt-et-un. Faites vos jeux.' Music emanated from the other side and she hurried towards the sound, brought up sharply by an attendant in evening dress.

'Your ticket, senhorita.' Quietly she explained, and he nodded. 'Senhor Rodriguez's table is at the far end of the floor. You can go in, but stay by the door until the cabaret is finished. It won't be long now.'

Lorna slipped through and breathed a sigh of relief. It was the first time she had entered the restaurant and she looked around with an interest tempered by impatience.

Manoel's table, directly opposite the band, was large and richly decorated with flowers, the men and women sitting round it still applauding the cabaret. She recognized the woman next to Manoel as the one she had seen with him in the car, and her eyes idly scanned the rest of the party, coming to rest incredulouly on a dark-haired man leaning towards the beautiful girl at his side. Inez and Rafael! What were they doing here? The beat of the music grew loud in her ears as she saw Inez smile directly into Rafael's eyes. Instinctively she turned to run, brought up short by the realization of why she was here. With an effort she turned back and made her way across the room.

Rafael saw her first and started to his feet. 'Lorna! What are you doing here?'

Ignoring him, she looked at Manoel. 'You are wanted at home, Senhor Rodriguez. Amalia is ill.'

Without waiting for a reply she turned on her heel and fled, reaching the exit before Manoel caught up with her.

'My car's outside,' he called. 'Come along.' Together they ran the last few steps, climbed into the roadster and roared up the hill.

'Tell me what happened,' he commanded. 'When did it start?'

Briefly she told him, and he heard her out in silence.

'I know what you are thinking,' he said when she had finished, 'and by God you're right! If anything happens to Amália I'll never forgive myself. Never!'

'It's rather late in the day for regret.' Lorna could not stop herself. 'You should have thought of that before.'

'I know. I deserve everything you say to me and more. If Amalia dies, I'll never be able to remember her without wishing I were dead, too!'

Lorna did not trust herself to reply to this extravagant outburst. It was time Manoel had a taste of his own medicine: a pity that in punishing him Amalia was the one to suffer!

They reached the house as the ambulance was drawing away, and reversing the car Manoel followed it to the nursing home on the other side of the town.

Together they kept vigil through the long reaches of the night, sitting on hard benches in the dimly lighted corridor. Nursing sisters glided past with a soft rustle, the rosaries at their waist clinking with the movement of their long white robes. By her side Manoel's lips moved in a continuous murmur of prayer, his face glistening with sweat, his eyes red-rimmed from anxiety and lack of sleep.

The first pale streaks of dawn were ushering in a new day when Doctor Zaldor came up to them, his white coat crumpled, the rubber gloves still on his hands.

'You wife is well, senhor,' he said slowly, 'and you have a son to be proud of. I will let you see them both for a moment.'

Left alone, Lorna cried quietly and thankfully: not only for her friend's happiness but for the death of her own. She leant her head against the window and looked at the lemon fingers of light that streaked the grey sky, dispersing clouds that lingered on the horizon. The immortal words of Browning came into her mind. 'God's in His heaven, All's right with the world.'

Yet her world was shattered. Difficult to believe that happiness for one person could bring disaster and disillusionment for another.

CHAPTER NINE

RETURNING home, Lorna went to her room and almost immediately fell into an exhausted sleep. The sun was high in the sky when she awoke and she lay in bed gazing at the light that penetrated the shutters and lay in ribs along the ceiling. She was reluctant to get up and face the problems ahead, but she resolutely dabbed cold water on her face and combed her hair back into a careless roll. As she moved her arm her engagement ring twisted round, and she took it off and held it ruminatively in her hand. The beautiful jewel had been a symbol of her future with Rafael. Now there was nothing, and with a sigh she slipped it into her pocket and went downstairs.

Laughter was coming from the library, and bracing herself she opened the door and went in. All the family, including Inez, were in the act of toasting Manoel.

'Ah, Lorna, you've come down just in time.' Rafael came forward with a brimming glass and she took it without looking directly at him. 'I did not want to disturb you earlier,' he murmured, 'but I'm glad you woke up in time to celebrate!'

Still she said nothing, and with a searching look he moved to the centre of the room and proposed a toast to his cousin.

Manoel responded with his usual gallantry and after extolling the beauty of the new arrival, concluded: 'Amalia and I have already decided on the name of our son.' He grinned and waved his arm. 'My son – how strange that sounds – but I'll get used to it, I suppose – my – son is to be called Francisco Pedro Rafael Fairfax Rodriguez.'

All eyes turned to Lorna and she swallowed hard. 'Thank you, Manoel. I – I never expected Amalia to in-

clude my family name. It was a lovely thought. Please tell
her for me.'

'I will.' The dark eyes were grave. 'If it had been a girl
we would have called her Lorna.'

'Oh no, you're embarrassing me. I did nothing.'

'But the nothing you did, you did so well!'

Everyone laughed and even the Senhora's face softened
into the semblance of a smile. 'The English coolness of
thought has much to commend it,' she said calmly.

'I wouldn't call the English cool,' Rosalia interposed.
'I think they build up a barrier so they can hide behind it!
Isn't that so, Lorna?'

Lorna's reply was cut short by Inez. 'Sometimes a
barrier is built to hide nothing.'

Rafael straightened, only the set of his mouth showing
his displeasure. 'This teasing is not in good taste. Lorna
was up most of the night and she is too tired for smart
repartee. I suggest we finish our drinks and then sit down
to lunch.'

Under cover of the general exodus he came to his
fiancée's side. 'There are storm clouds in your eyes, my
dearest. What does it presage?'

'Nothing,' Lorna said calmly. 'The storm has finished
and the sea is calm.'

The breath hissed sharply between his teeth. 'You have
a nasty habit of hitting below the belt.'

'Let go my arm : you're hurting me!'

'Good. That's what you are doing to me by your inability to see further than your stupid, turned-up nose.'
Smiling as tenderly as if he had been whispering sweet
nothings, he seated her at the dining-room table and then
turned solicitously towards his mother. 'How does it feel
to be a great-aunt, Mama?'

'Wonderful. We need a baby in the house. A pity it will
be for such a short time, though. Must Amalia go back to
Brazil so soon?'

'Yes. It is all arranged.'

'But surely—'

'No, Mother, everything is settled.'

The Senhora's face grew mutinous and her son put his hand on the thin shoulder. 'Don't worry, *cara*, there will soon be babies of mine to bring laughter here! Is that not so, Lorna?'

A red tide of colour swept into Lorna's face and she bent silently over her plate. Rafael gazed at her for an instant, his eyes mocking, before he turned back to his food.

The high spirits of the family continued through lunch. Conversation was mainly in Portuguese which Lorna only followed with difficulty, and she was aware that in this moment of rejoicing she stood outside the family circle. Everyone teased Manoel as if he were the only person who had produced little Francisco, and she found it difficult to restrain herself when he was toasted for the third time. In his grey suit he looked, she thought, like a pouter pigeon, puffing out his chest as if it were his plumage!

'I expect you find our customs strange.' Inez spoke to Lorna, her voice pitched low so that no one else could hear. 'No doubt you are thinking Amalia should come into this somewhere.'

'As a matter of fact I was,' Lorna said frankly. 'The woman's part seems to be taken too much for granted.'

'It is – but Portuguese women do not mind. I can see that for you it would be difficult.'

'You see too much, Miss Castro. It is not always a good thing.'

'Neither is it a good thing not to see enough. You have a proverb which says there is none so blind as those who will not see.' Inez smoothed her hair and deliberately changed the conversation. 'Your arrival at the Casino last night was a little unexpected.'

'I'm sorry I disturbed you.'

'*Ça ne fait rien.* I only hope you were not jealous to find me with Rafael.'

Lorna's hand tightened on her fork and she knew a mad impulse to throw it at the smiling girl next to her. "Why should I be jealous? After all, one evening is so little compared with a lifetime!'

There was no reply, and Lorna turned back to her dessert, conscious of having won a bitter victory.

They were sipping coffee in the drawing-room when Rafael broke the news that a man would be coming for dinner that evening. The manner in which he spoke implied that this was no chance visitor, and Lorna followed his glance to where it rested on Rosalia. Enlightenment dawned; Rafael obviously thought it was time to find his sister a suitable husband!

'Who is he?' Rosalia was on the alert. 'Do I know him?'

'No, he is from Oporto, but I have known him since his marriage.'

The girl relaxed. 'He's married, then?'

'He is a widower.'

'Oh! You're not—'

'And you are a widow.' Forestalling further argument, he stood up. 'How about a drive – all of you? We could do with some fresh air.'

'I'd rather rest in the garden,' Lorna said quickly. 'But you go by all means.'

'I've no intention of going without you. A drive will do you good.'

She stood up and moved past him. 'You recommend it as the panacea of all ills. I don't know what you'd do if you didn't have a car.'

'Use an aeroplane! Now don't argue with me, Lorna. I'm never at a loss for words, you should know that by now.'

Setting her lips, Lorna went upstairs, slipped on a coat and defiantly refusing to make herself look more presentable, went down to the car. Inez and Rosalia were already inside and she slipped into the seat beside Rafael.

' "Once more into the breach, dear friends",' she quoted softly. 'Where are we going this time?'

'I've a good mind not to tell you.' His voice was polite, but his knuckles gleamed white on the wheel. 'You're the most infuriating woman I know. One day I will teach you a lesson.'

She did not reply and he went on: 'We're going to Nazare. It's one of the loveliest places in Europe and its inhabitants are supposed to be descendants of the original Phoenicians.'

'You sound like a guide book.'

'I thought you'd prefer it to my talking like a lover!'

'Talking means nothing. If you acted like one it would be more appropriate.'

'And what am I supposed to gauge from that?'

'What you like. I don't care.'

He set his jaw, and Lorna stared fixedly out of the window.

As if sensing the discord between them Inez kept leaning forward to talk to Rafael, her mouth almost touching his ear, her breath warm on his cheek. Lorna could smell the perfume she wore, see the fine pores of the skin and the golden flecks in her eyes, and she turned her head away and stared moodily out of the window.

They were approaching Nazare and everywhere were great splashes of colour. The little village was given over to fishing and the gaily dressed population thronged the broad beach and the promenade behind it. Women sat beside rush mats covered with salt fish drying in the sun, their full skirts spread out around them, gold earrings flashing as they chattered. Children ran over the sand; the older boys were busy mending fishing nets and oxen slept or ruminated between the brightly painted boats which were as picturesque as the people, with long prows terminating in high, sharp points.

Rafael parked the car near the beach and they climbed out and walked along the seafront. The sun was low in the sky and a group of women crouched in a dark circle on the white sand, their black shawls hiding their gay skirts as they awaited the return of the boats round the headland of the bay. The whole scene had peace and dignity and a strange remoteness from the outer world.

Lorna jumped down on to the sand. 'Come along, Rosalia, let's have a look at the boats.'

'Not me; thanks. I can't bear sand in my shoes. Inez and I will walk up here.'

Throwing his sister a grateful glance, Rafael leapt lightly on to the beach and caught Lorna's hand. 'We'll take a little walk,' he said softly. 'Don't argue with me, please. I am not in the mood.'

Holding her hand in a vice-like grip, he propelled her along the beach, keeping up a fast pace until they had left the crowds behind and were alone in a world of sun and sand and water.

He slowed down and surveyed her. 'Now we can talk. I suppose your anger is because you're imagining completely erroneous things about last night?'

'I couldn't care less about last night. What you do is no concern of mine.'

'How can you say that?' he flared out. 'We are engaged. Everything that I do is your concern in the same way that everything you do is my concern.'

'Don't shout at me!'

'I'd like to do more than just shout at you! Never have I met a woman who can be so maddening. Do you purposely want to misunderstand in order to hurt me?'

'Hurt *you*!' She was incensed. 'What about you hurting me?'

'I've never wittingly hurt you in my life.'

'Then we don't agree on what constitutes a hurt.'

'It appears we don't agree on a lot of things,' he said

coldly. 'For my part I think I am the one who should be annoyed.'

'What in heaven's name have you got to be annoyed at?'

'Everything. You misjudged me once before, but I never thought you'd do so again. Why do you always jump to the wrong conclusion? Have you no faith in me?'

'What am I supposed to think when I see you sitting in the Casino with Inez? Was that your business dinner?'

'It was.' He struck his hands in his pockets. 'The men were passing through Lisbon on their way to Brazil and I intended taking them to a restaurant in town. However, they wanted to gamble, so we dined first in the Casino restaurant.'

'With Inez, I suppose?'

'She happened to be there with her cousin and joined our table.'

'And your business discussion? — or was that unimportant compared with the pleasure of being with the lovely Miss Castro?'

'Damn it, Lorna, this inquisition is intolerable! You don't deserve an answer!'

'Don't give one, then — it wouldn't worry me!'

'On the contrary, I think it would worry you a great deal.' His humour returned and with it his equanimity. 'If you were not blinded by jealousy you wouldn't see things out of proportion.'

'You flatter yourself.'

'A good thing. You certainly don't do it for me!' He caught her none too gently by the shoulder. 'I thought you would be sure of me by now, *querida*, yet you're still as uncertain as when we first met. Don't you know that you don't always dine with business colleagues to discuss business? More contracts are made over a good meal and a bottle of wine than any office desk. When I saw how the evening was going I almost telephoned to ask you down, only I knew you wouldn't want to leave Amalia.'

'That's as good an excuse as any.'

'It's not an excuse,' he said angrily. 'You've said your-self that you've not spent enough time with her. How was I to know you'd want to come?'

'I didn't. I wouldn't be seen dead in public with any of Manoel's friends! You may not have any scruples, Rafael, but I have.'

Her thrust went home and his face darkened. 'I deserve that. But I had no choice in the matter. Manoel was already there and I couldn't ignore him; it would have caused too much gossip.'

'Don't you think people are already talking about him? It's common knowledge the way he's been carrying on — everyone knows it — including Amalia! You should think about me for a change instead of your family! How do you think I felt when I discovered you at the Casino!'

'How was I to know you'd be coming?'

'Did you intend keeping it a secret?'

'*Comos Diabos!* Are you purposely trying to mis-understand? What's the matter with you, Lorna, do you want to start a quarrel?' His hand crushed hers and suddenly he lifted it up. 'Where's your ring?'

Without a word she took it from her pocket and held it out. 'It's yours, Rafael, you'd better have it.'

'I don't understand.'

'It's quite simple — I'm breaking off our engagement.'

'Don't be absurd. I refuse to let you go. You're not dealing with a child, Lorna. I'm a man, and it's time you grew up and behaved more like a woman!'

'It's because I'm a woman that I don't want your ring.'

The lines on either side of his mouth deepened and he looked down speculatively at the pearl.

> "*O homen fogo, a mulher est opa,*
> *Vem o dibao e assop ra.*"

'I don't understand you.' Her voice was cold.

'"Man is fire and woman tow — the devil comes and starts to blow!" It's an ancient proverb and very apt.' His tone changed. 'But I'm stupid to treat you seriously. I ought to put you across my knee and spank all this nonsense out of you, it's the only way to make you see sense!'

'You wouldn't get a second opportunity!'

'I wouldn't need one!'

For a moment she was speechless, then her lips quivered and she threw herself against him. 'Oh, Rafael,' he said brokenly, 'I can't bear it when we quarrel!'

He held her close. 'Neither can I, *querida*. Why must you keep torturing me with your distrust?' He slipped the ring on her finger and held her hand against his lips. 'I won't put this on a third time, Lorna. I love you too much to keep fighting you.'

'Oh, Rafael, I didn't mean to hurt you.'

'I know, but you do so nonetheless.' He rubbed his cheek against hers. 'It will be better when we're married,' he said softly. 'Once you're mine you won't be afraid of anyone coming between us. We'll put up the banns as soon as I come back from Africa.'

'You're going away?'

'I'm afraid so, dearest. It's something I must attend to myself. I'd hoped we would have been married by now, in which case you could have come with me. As it is . . .' He put his arm over her shoulder. 'I hate leaving you, *cara*; every day we're apart will be an eternity.'

She rested her head on his chest and felt his heart pounding against her ear. The warmth of his body enveloped her and she put her arms round his neck.

'I wish you didn't have to go, Rafael. I'm afraid.'

'There's nothing to be afraid of, darling.'

'Not when you're with me. It's when I'm alone that I feel so alien.'

'You can't feel alien in my home.'

'I do. I feel they don't want me.'

'Nonsense! You're imagining things. Everything has happened too quickly, that's all. Once we've settled down together things will right themselves.'

'If only I could be sure of that! Oh, Rafael, I've tried so hard to make you understand what I feel – but you won't listen.'

'Are you afraid you don't love me enough – is that what is is?'

She shook her head. 'That I love you too much to accept only half of you.'

He smiled. 'And who do you think will get the other half?'

'I'm serious, Rafael.' She moved away from the oblivion of his arms. 'I know I'm putting it badly, but I've got to be sure that marriage means the same to you as it does to me.'

'And what does it mean to you?'

'Everything. Sharing ideas, companionship understanding.'

'And love?' he said quietly. 'Surely that should come first.'

'Love isn't enough by itself.'

'If it's big enough it is. Oh, Lorna, why won't you accept today for what it is and stop probing into the future?'

'Because our marriage is part of the future! It isn't built on today, on one moment. It's built up of years of understanding and pulling together, and I've got to be sure we're not pulling different ways.'

'I thought you were sure.'

'I'm not. Not any more.'

'I see.' He moved over to the edge of the ocean and stared out at the far horizon. There was no sound except the plop, plop of the waves on the sand and the sibilant rush of the receding water.

'Do you remember the story of Ruth?' he said without turning round. ' "Whither thou goest I will go, thy people shall be my people!'" That's how I feel about you, and I thought you felt the same way about me.'

'But you're not giving up your home and country for me!'

He turned, his eyes grave. 'Would you believe me if I said I would?'

'I don't know.'

'Ah,' the sound was like a sigh. 'I'm glad you told me the truth. At least we can be honest with one another.' He took out a cigarette and tapped it thoughtfully on the back of his hand. 'In my opinion you're more afraid of marriage than of losing your nationality. You see Manoel and Amalia as a typical Portuguese couple and you keep thinking of all the sordid intrigues that go on behind the scenes. But men have mistresses in New York and London too, don't forget that. I don't throw up all the English marriages that end in divorce, or worry because your countrywomen are considered cold and sexless. I love you and I'm willing to take a chance, and you've got to feel the same way about me. You must take me as I am.'

'But who are you?' She flung out her hands helplessly. 'Do you want to share your life with me or keep me in the background as someone to come home to?' Tears poured down her cheeks and she dashed them away. 'I want to believe you, Rafael; I want to go wherever you go, but I can't if I don't know where the road is leading!'

'Does it matter as long as we're together?' In two strides he bridged the gap between them and took her in his arms. Tenderly he wiped away her tears and stroked back the hair from her temples. 'You must trust me, Lorna. You must believe that I'll do anything in the world to protect you and that your happiness comes before mine.'

'I do trust you, Rafael.'

'Then there's nothing more to be said.'

He bent his head and laid his mouth on hers. There was no passion in his touch, only a deep sympathy, signifying protection instead of mastery, a desire to give rather than to take.

It was dusk when they returned to the car, to be met by a twinkling-eyed Rosalia and sullen Inez. But Lorna was impervious to anyone except Rafael and during the drive home sat close by his side, her body touching his, the muscle of his leg hard against hers. For the first time since their engagement she was at peace and resolutely refused to wonder how long it would last.

That night there was a small dinner party for the young widower from Oporto. Throughout the meal Rosalia was shy and withdrawn, and her great dark eyes would rest on the man, only to slide away the minute he looked in her direction.

Oliveira Deveer was a slim, suave man in his early forties with an ascetic yet genial face. Lorna could imagine him in a monk's cowl riding with Chaucer's pilgrims to Canterbury, and during dinner he revealed himself as good a raconteur as the Prioress or the Man of Law.

In the drawing-room again Senhor Deveer approached Lorna. 'May I congratulate you on your engagement, senhorita? I think Rafael is very fortunate.'

His eyes were friendly and Lorna smiled her thanks.

'And what do you say to our country?' he continued. 'You like it?'

'Very much. It's so colourful and gay – quite different from the grey streets of London.'

'And much warmer too! I am always glad to get back to the Portuguese sunshine whenever I go to England.' He sat down on the seat next to her. 'Have you been to Oporto yet? Oh, then that's a treat in store for you. You must persuade Rafael to bring you along; it is well worth a visit.'

'You live in the city, senhor?'

'A few miles outside – children need plenty of room to expand!' He drew out his wallet and proudly handed her a snapshot of two dark-haired youngsters. 'This is

Pedro – he's the wicked one of the family – and that is Juan, the dreamer, he is always as solemn as an owl.'

'They look very sweet. How old are they?'

'Eight and five. My wife died when Juan was born.'

Lorna murmured sympathetically, and he sighed. 'Yes, the ways of God are strange. She was very much like Senhora' – he smiled apologetically, 'I am afraid I don't know her married name – Senhorita Rodriguez; she had the same movements and gentle expression.'

'It must be heartbreaking for you to see her, then.'

'Oh no, it brings back happy memories. I met the Senhorita when she was engaged to Juan Diniz, but of course she doesn't remember me.' Something in his voice made Lorna look at him more fully. He was not as suave as she had imagined : there was a sadness lurking behind his eyes that touched her.

'Do you think she has changed much?' Lorna asked curiously.

'No. She's as lovely as ever – lovelier, in fact : sadness has given her a grace and dignity she never possessed before. Do you think she's happy?'

'Why do you ask me?'

'Because you are *"sympathique"*. You sense things without being told.' He leaned forward in his chair. 'You of all people should know whether she is contented here, whether she has recovered from the loss of her husband.'

Lorna shook her head. 'If there's anything you want to know about Rosalia you must ask Rosalia herself, or else Rafael. He's better qualified to tell you than I am.'

He smiled. 'I admire your tact, but a brother sees so much and no more! When I heard Rosalia had come back to Portugal I decided to try my luck with her. I came down to see Rafael and told him of my desire to marry his sister.'

Still unused to the Latin habit of frankness about their emotions, Lorna tried not to show her surprise. 'Why didn't you do so earlier, senhor – before she was engaged to Juan, I mean?'

'There was no point. Why should a young girl want a widower with two children? But things are different now. At least I hope so.' He stood up. 'Shall we go over and talk to her? I see her glancing in our direction.'

'You don't need me. I'm sure you'll do better alone!'

'But I am shy!'

Lorna burst out laughing and out of the corner of her eye saw Rosalia watching them curiously. 'Go on over,' she whispered, 'and good luck!'

With a little bow he moved purposefully across the room to Rosalia's side.

Soon they were close in conversation, his voice low and intimate and Rosalia's eyelids fluttering, the dimple in her cheeks coming and going.

Everyone in the room breathed a sigh of relief, and Lorna intercepted a look between mother and son that told of great satisfaction. Rafael sauntered over and sat down on the settee at her side.

'What do you think of my match-making?'

'Sheer genius! I'm not surprised you're smug when everyone falls in with your plans so readily. Think anything will come of it?'

'Of course. I give them two months at the most, and Rosalia will be queening it over the ladies of Oporto! Oliveira is a good fellow too, he will know how to handle her.'

'Handle her?'

'Naturally. A well-bred woman is like a racehorse, high-spirited and lively but responsive to the touch! Like you, my darling.' He leaned against her. '*Diabos!* I wish I weren't going tomorrow. If only I could have postponed the trip we could have got married and gone together.'

'But you'll be back soon.'

'As soon as I can get away.' His fingers interlocked

with hers. 'Let's go into the garden, Lorna, I'm aching to hold you in my arms.'

It was with a deep sense of loneliness that Lorna stood on the steps the following morning and waved Rafael good-bye. With Amalia in hospital she would feel more isolated than ever – a fact the Senhora would be quick to notice and act on. She sighed and turned back into the hall, surprised to find Inez watching her, exquisite in a turquoise suit, her dark hair twisted in a coronet on her head.

'You're looking pale, Lorna. Has Rafael gone?'

'Yes.'

'How annoying! I wanted to see him before he went.'

Disinclined for verbal battle, Lorna curbed her curiosity and began to walk past, but Inez held out her hand to display an exquisite pair of jade earrings.

'He promised to bring me back a bracelet to match and I wanted him to get the colour exactly right. Do you think I could catch him at the airport?'

'I doubt it,' Lorna said coldly. 'Besides, he'll be too busy to think about buying anything.'

'He wasn't too busy to bring me the earrings.' Inez's voice was deceptively sweet. 'As a matter of fact he suggested getting the bracelet himself. But I suppose in the rush he forgot to ask me for the earrings.' She smiled deprecatingly. 'Oh well, it can't be helped. Another time perhaps.'

'Not if I have anything to do with it!' Lorna lost her temper. 'You should find a man of your own to buy you presents.'

'I had one until you came along and stole him!'

'I couldn't steal something you never possessed!'

There was an ugly silence and Inez arched her back like a cat. 'Believe what you want, Lorna. One day you'll wake up to the truth.'

'And so will you. Rafael's engaged to me, yet you're stupid enough to think you can come between us with your veiled hints and lies.'

'Indeed!' A faint flush tinged Inez's skin. 'I can't believe you're as innocent as you pretend. Surely you don't think you can make Rafael happy for long? I'll admit that at the moment you're a novelty to him, but wait until you try entertaining his friends with your stumbling Portuguese; wait until he starts taking you for granted and expectes you to sit at home while he goes out. *Diabos,* you don't know what you're letting yourself in for! You weren't brought up to live my sort of life and you'll get so bored you'll want to run away.'

'You'd like to think so, wouldn't you? Well, you can't make me run away so easily.'

'I won't have to try,' Inez said rudely. 'Time will do it for me!'

Lorna drew back. 'If you've quite finished I'd like you to go.'

'I'll be glad to.' Inez turned on her heel, but at the door she paused and looked back. 'Strange as it may seem I don't dislike you as much as I thought. I always admire a fighter even when they're fighting a lost cause!'

Left alone, Lorna sank down on a chair and buried her head in her hands. More than ever she needed Rafael to assure her that everything would be all right, that Inez had only spoken from jealousy and hate. How fragile was her confidence if it could be shattered by a few jealous words!

That evening she went to see Amalia, amazed at the transformation in her friend. Her hair shone, her skin glowed and her eyes sparkled. She was sitting up in bed, a lace bedjacket over her shoulder and Francisco lying beside her in his crib. Lorna looked down at the tiny, perfect face, the straight hair sticking up like a porcupine from the round head, a smudge of an eyebrow and small fat nose and mouth. Gently she touched one hand, marvelling at the myriad lines that made it look as if he had toiled for centuries. Her throat contracted and she turned to Amalia with tears in her eyes.

'He's wonderful, darling. The most adorable baby ever!'

The happy mother looked suitably modest. 'He is rather sweet, isn't he? The nurse told me he's the handsomest baby that's been born here.' She leaned over and peered into the crib. 'You are, aren't you, my precious? And such a temper!'

Lorna smiled dutifully as Amalia launched into details of the baby's diet and habits, the words skimming across the surface of her brain as she murmured the appropriate answers.

That night Lorna dined alone with the Senhora. It was not a very happy meal and they had reached dessert before the old lady spoke.

'It was unnecessary of you to quarrel with Inez, my dear. Differences of opinion cannot be resolved with rudeness.'

'Differences of opinion is a polite way of putting it,' Lorna said quietly. 'I can think of a much more suitable name.'

'Such as?'

'Jealousy. It is quite obvious Inez expected Rafael to marry her and she doesn't take kindly to the idea of being superseded.'

The Senhora went on calmly peeling a peach. 'Perhaps Inez had good reason to think so.'

'If you're trying to insinuate that Rafael said anything to her . . .'

'A man does not always have to put things into words. Quite often a woman bases her reasoning on what he does *not* say.'

'I should hardly think Rafael ever suffered from an inability to express himself! He had ample opportunity to marry Inez before I arrived – the fact that he fell in love with me is proof that she meant nothing to him.'

'I cannot agree with you there. Sometimes the most sensible men do not see what is under their nose, nor do they realize what they are missing until they have lost it.'

'Rafael doesn't look as if he's lost anything,' Lorna said shortly. 'He's perfectly happy. At least he would be if you didn't make your dislike quite so apparent. You were so nice to me when I came here, senhora. Why should you be different now?'

'Because everything is different. You came as Amalia's companion, not as a future wife to my son. You might twist him round your little finger, but you cannot tell me what to do. I am an old lady and entitled to my opinions whether or not they concur with yours.'

'I'm not trying to make you alter your opinions,' Lorna said desperately. 'It's only that it seems a pity for us not to be friends.'

'We can never be friends,' the Senhora grunted.

'Why not? And even if we can't there's still no reason for us to quarrel. I've gone out of my way to be polite to you. I know you find it hard to welcome another woman into your home, but you can't keep your son all the time!'

'I don't want to keep him all the time. You are misconstruing the reasons for my disapproval.'

. 'If you're going to repeat what you told me in front of Amalia I don't want to hear.' Lorna flung down her napkin. 'Although while we're trying to clear the air a bit it might be as well if I told you that I'd appreciate your not asking Inez here in future.'

'I'm not in the habit of taking orders from anyone! This is still my home and I will do as I see fit. When you are married will be time enough for you to take the reins in your own hands.'

Lorna did not reply to this and the meal was finished to painful silence.

At the end of the week Rosalia left to visit her aunt in Oporto. With some amusement Lorna sat on the bed and watched her pack, thinking how fortunate it was to have relations wherever they were needed!

With Rosalia away the house seemed more desolate

than ever, and Lorna's boredom increased. Rafael was an intermittent correspondent and the few letters she received were lifeless and utterly lacking in warmth and personality. There was nothing in common between the passionate man she knew and the sender of these stereotyped tracts.

A fortnight later Lorna was sitting alone in the drawing room after dinner, struggling with her Portuguese grammar, when the shrilling of the telephone cut across her thoughts. Not waiting for the maid to answer it, she walked into the library and lifted the receiver. It was Rafael.

Her knees grew weak and she sat down abruptly.

'Rafael darling! What a lovely surprise. How are you?'

'Much better now I can hear your voice again. My God, Lorna, I never knew I could miss you so much! It's taking me twice as long to settle things because I can't get you out of my mind.'

Her laughter trembled on the verge of tears. 'Oh, darling, don't say that. I can't bear you to stay away a day longer than necessary.'

'Don't worry, I won't. How's Mother?'

'Very well. Would you like to speak to her?'

'No, I only wanted to hear your voice again. Letters are so inadequate. What did you say? The line's terrible darling. I can't hear you.'

'Your letters aren't a bit like you,' she shouted.

'Neither are yours, but we won't have to rely on them much longer. I'll be back at the end of the month.'

The operator's voice cut in, and there was a muttered imprecation in Portuguese.

'I've got to go now, Lorna. They won't let me speak any longer. Take care of yourself, my dearest.'

'I will. And you do the same.'

'I can't hear you.'

'Nothing. Nothing. Oh, Rafael darling —' but the line

was already dead, and with an overwhelming sense of depression she replaced the receiver. There was so much she had wanted to hear, so much that had been left unsaid she almost wished he had not telephoned at all. With a sigh she turned off the light and walked up the stairs to tell the Senhora.

The woman was sitting in an easy chair by the window, a piece of petit-point in her hand.

'Good evening, Lorna. Come in.'

'I hope I'm not disturbing you.'

'Not at all. I thought you were with Amalia.'

'I saw her this morning.' Lorna sat down on the edge of a chair. 'Rafael just telephoned.'

The Senhora looked up. 'Is he on the line?'

'No, he was only able to speak for a few minutes. He sent you his love.'

'Thank you. I would have preferred to have spoken to him myself.'

There was an awkward silence. 'Did he say when he would be coming back?' the old lady spoke again.

'At the end of the month. When is Rosalia returning?'

'Probably the same time.'

'I see.' There was another pause and Lorna bridged it uneasily. 'It'll be a good thing when she's married to Senhor Deveer, although I daresay you'll miss her.'

'Who told you about the marriage?'

'Rosalia. And Rafael in the beginning, of course.'

'I thought no one outside the family knew.'

Lorna bit her lip. 'I'll be one of the family soon.'

'Unfortunately I cannot forget that. I —'

'Please, senhora, don't go on. You've already told me what you think. You need not do so again.'

'But I cannot stand by and see my son's life ruined!'

'Why should I ruin Rafael? I love him – love him so much I'd do anything rather than harm him. Why do you keep saying he won't be happy with me?'

'Because I'm old enough to see a little further into the

T—F

future than you, old enough to know that people don't change merely because you want them to.'

'But I don't want him to change. I love him as he is.'

'You are lying!'

'I'm not!'

'You are!' The Senhora swept her embroidery to the floor. 'Even before you are married you want to change him. Do you think that once you're his wife you'll be content to leave him as he is? Oh, I know what's been going on in your mind even though I haven't said anything about it before — but you can't go on like this, your conflict won't resolve itself in marriage.'

'You can't say that,' Lorna protested. 'You can't bludgeon me into believing what you want me to believe.'

'I don't intend to. If you are honest you will see it for yourself. You're different from us, Lorna. No matter how hard you try you will never be able to accept our ideas, our customs or our way of life, any more than we could accept yours.'

'Why should it make any difference? Why can't Rafael and I be happy without giving up our heritage?'

'Because no marriage can succeed where husband and wife don't share the same beliefs.'

'There's such a thing as give and take.'

'Not with Rafael! I love my son, but I know him too. Either you will have to change or ...'

'I won't listen to you. You're trying to make me afraid. You're putting ideas in my head.'

'They were there long before I spoke. I am merely formulating them.'

'No, no! They weren't — not so clearly. I know Rafael and I are different — I won't argue about that — but it's a difference that won't mean anything in time. Our marriage *will* work, I tell you! Our love is big enough to overcome any obstacles.'

'You must believe what you think fit and allow me to

do the same.' The Senhora picked up her petit-point and smoothed it on her lap. 'Don't think I'm speaking like this because I am jealous. If the circumstances were different you would be a good wife for my son. As it is you will never be happy together. For a few years, maybe – but when the first passion wears off, what will you have to take its place?'

'Understanding.'

'Never. You're just mouthing words you'd like to believe. Rafael doesn't understand you any more than you understand him.'

Abruptly Lorna moved over to the Senhora's side. 'What would you advise me to do?'

'What your heart tells you.'

'But that's just it – I don't know! One minute I think it'd be better if I went away and the next I can't bear the thought of leaving him. Rafael's my life, I tell you. I can't give him up, I can't!'

'But you want his happiness?'

'More than my own.'

'In that case you should go. Go while you still have the chance. It's the only thing to do. You are young with your whole life ahead of you, and in a few months you will forget.'

'Never!'

'Yes, you will. Once you are in England everything here will seem like a dream.'

'And will Rafael forget too?'

'Of course.' The black eyes were expressionless. 'The man is not born who remembers for ever. At first he will be hurt and angry, but soon he will come to see that you did the only thing possible and then ...'

'Then he'll turn to Inez.' Lorna's breath was a sob. 'It's what you want, isn't it?'

The woman picked up her embroidery. 'Inez is right for him as you can never be.'

'That's not true! Many people of different nationalities

are happily married. Why should ours be the only one to fail?'

'It wouldn't be.' The needle flashed, its long coloured tail winding in and out of the canvas, 'Look at your compatriots who married Americans. How many of those marriages succeeded? Yet there is more affinity between your country and the United States than there is between you and Portugal.'

'I still think you're distorting things. I know what you say is true, but I'm sure there's an answer for every one of your arguments.' Lorna was trembling so violently it was difficult to talk. 'I'm not the right person to argue with you, senhora. I've worried so much that my brain goes round and round until I can't think clearly any more, and that's the truth.'

'There's nothing to think about,' the woman said firmly. 'Go home before it's too late. If you love Rafael you must leave him. It's the only way.'

Tears poured down Lorna's cheeks and the room blurred and distorted so that the Senhora loomed larger. 'I can't believe it,' she sobbed. 'There must be another solution.'

'There isn't. Take my advice and go back where you are wanted.'

'Rafael wants me!'

'He *thinks* he does.'

There was no sound in the room except the ticking of the grandfather clock in the corner, each beat repeating the Senhora's words : 'Go home. Tick-tock. Go home.'

Lifelessly Lorna stood up. 'You win,' she said indistinctly. 'I'll go home. You're a selfish, bigoted old woman, but I believe you put your children's happiness first.'

'I can assure you I do. You are doing the right thing, my dear. One day you will thank me.'

'Never that. Never that, whatever happens.' Without another word Lorna turned on her heel and ran out of the room.

CHAPTER TEN

LORNA spent a sleepless night going over in her mind everything the Senhora had said. There was no answer to the old lady's arguments. Time alone would prove whether she was right or wrong, and to take a chance and marry Rafael was more than she dared do. If she did not love him so much it would be easy to take her own happiness, but the knowledge that by doing so she might wreck his future was more than she could bear. Their love had been wrong from the start. It had been born from the differences between them, differences that had at first repelled and then attracted them so violently that they were both helplessly enmeshed in a passion that bore no logical thought.

As early as she could she left the house and went down to Cook's. Her mind was made up and to delay now would serve no useful purpose. She dared not wait to see Rafael: one glance at his face, a touch of his hand and her resolve would weaken. Better to leave while she still had the strength of mind.

To her dismay the man in Cook's office shook his head when he heard that she wanted to leave immediately.

'The planes are booked up for at least two weeks.'

'But that's impossible!'

'It's true none the less. There are only three flights a week from Lisbon to London, and one of them is the BOAC plane from South America. It stops here before going to England.' He thumbed the page of the book in front of him. 'There's always a chance that one or two passengers will get off at Lisbon, but we couldn't let you know in advance. You'd have to wait until the plane landed, or we might possibly be able to give you a couple of hours' notice.'

'What about Portuguese Airlines?'

'Also booked up.' He picked his teeth and surveyed her. 'Of course there's always a chance of a cancellation there too. If you'll give me your phone number I'll give you a ring when I get one in.'

'I can't do that. I must know definitely one way or the other when I can leave. Isn't there any other means of getting out of Portugal?'

'There's always the train, but I wouldn't recommend it. It's not bad if you're travelling with a party of people, but not on your own.' He snapped his fingers. 'I've got it! You can go by boat. There are any number of steamers plying between here and London. Wait a minute and I'll find out if there's a berth.'

Lorna sat down on a bench against the wall and listened to the man speaking into the telephone. The spate of Portuguese that followed was evidently satisfactory for he replaced the receiver and smiled.

'The *Fernandez* leaves Lisbon at five a.m. tomorrow and they have room for one more passenger. It's not a luxury liner, you understand, but they carry ten or twelve passengers and you'll only have to share your cabin with one other woman.'

Lorna moved over to the counter, her hands shaking so much it was difficult to search in her bag for her traveller's cheques. Incredible to think that this time tomorrow she would be on the ocean, miles away from Portugal and Rafael!

'Well,' the man said sharply, 'will you take it? I've got to ring them back right away.'

'Yes – yes, I will.'

Within half an hour all the formalities were concluded and it was barely eleven o'clock when she left Cook's office and walked out into the arcade. The only thing left to do was to pack and say good-bye to Amalia.

Amalia was delighted to see her. 'This is a surprise! What brings you here so early?' At the expression on

Lorna's face her own lost its smile. 'Darling, you look terrible! What's the matter?'

'I'm going home.'

'Is your aunt ill?'

'It's got nothing to do with my aunt. This is between me and Rafael. I can't marry him.'

'Oh, Lorna, I didn't know you'd quarrelled! When did he get back?'

Lorna pushed back her hair and stood up nervously. 'He isn't back. He's still away: I can't marry him, that's all.'

Amalia stared in consternation. 'I don't know what you're talking about! I thought you were so happy. You can't tell me you've stopped loving him, because I won't believe it.'

'I'll never stop loving him,' Lorna said wearily. 'I only feel it isn't the right sort of love.'

'Is there a wrong sort?'

'At one time I wouldn't have thought so, but now I'm not so sure. Sometimes a passion can burn so deeply it destroys everything it touches and creates nothing.'

Amalia shuddered. 'You sound like Edgar Allan Poe! It's unlike you to be melodramatic. Are you sure you feel well?'

Lorna managed a brittle laugh. 'Perfectly. I think that for the first time I've found the courage to act on my convictions. I've been uncertain for a long time — you know that — and it's only now I've found the strength to go through with it.'

'Have you talked it over with anyone else?'

'Senhora Rodriguez.'

'I might have guessed she was behind it all! How stupid to take any notice of anything she's put into your mind.'

'She hasn't put anything into my mind. She's only helped me to clarify what's there.'

'Well, I don't think it will remain there once Rafael's had a chance to talk to you.'

Lorna stood up and moved over to the window. 'I'm not going to give him the opportunity.'

'What do you mean?'

'I'm leaving tomorrow.'

'But you can't! You can't go without seeing him — it isn't fair!'

Lorna's voice was thick with unshed tears. 'I must. If I don't it will be too late. It isn't easy for me to go, Amalia, for God's sake don't make it any harder!'

Amalia sank back on the pillows. 'I never dreamt you'd do a thing like this. Oh, I knew you were worried — anyone could see that — but I didn't think it was serious enough to make you break off your engagement. I could swear that you loved him—'

'I do, with all my heart.'

'Then why run away?'

'Because it wouldn't work out.' Lorna moved over to the bed. 'Please, Amalia, be honest with me. You're sorry I'm leaving, but you can't truthfully tell me I'm wrong to go.'

'I'd be afraid to. I'd like nothing better than for you to marry Rafael — you know that — but I've learnt enough in the past year to realize you can't make people fit into patterns just because you want them to. You and Rafael are so different that I'm not surprised you have doubts. He's a man who will never conform to any standards. He has his own code of ethics and will expect the woman he loves to live up to them. He's a born Lord of the Manor, and you can never alter him in that respect.'

'It isn't only Rafael — it's the country and everything else.'

Amalia smiled bitterly. 'You needn't explain. I don't blame you for not wanting to live here. Portugal's wonderful as long as you're willing to accept its customs and beliefs. But you can't accept them any more than I can.'

'That's why you're going to Brazil!'

'And that's why you're returning to England.'

'Then you agree I'm doing the right thing?'

'I don't think you're doing the wrong thing. Whether or not it's the only thing I wouldn't like to say. As things are now you'd find Rafael's circle too artificial to satisfy you. You'd fight every inch of the way and in the end you'd find you were fighting Rafael too.'

Amalia shifted her position slightly. 'But why don't you wait and see Rafael first? I don't think it's fair to leave him without giving him a chance to see if you can work something out between you.'

Lorna's eyes were anguished. 'Rafael would only answer me with kisses. And no woman who loves him could fight against those.' She turned away. 'I daren't see him!'

There was a puzzled frown on Amalia's face. 'Are you sure you aren't running away because you're afraid of him?'

'What do you mean?'

'Only that he's a man who'll take a lot of living up to. He doesn't know the meaning of the word compromise; he'll give a lot, but he'll expect a lot in return.'

'And I'd willingly give him everything he'd expect! No woman could deny Rafael anything.' With one hand Lorna pleated the counterpane. 'I'll admit that I was afraid of him in the beginning, but not now. I'm afraid of myself, Amalia, afraid that I won't have the strength of mind to live up to my principles. If I marry him I'll become a puppet agreeing with everything he says, believing everything he tells me because my desire to please him will be stronger than my desire to please myself.' Her voice broke. 'I wanted my marriage to be a partnership, but I don't think Rafael knows the meaning of the word. I'm not criticizing him,' she said passionately. 'He was brought up that way. Only it's a way of life that would destroy us both in the end.'

'Perhaps he'll alter when you're married?'

'Oh, Amalia, it's hopeless. You said yourself you should never marry and expect people to change.'

'Have you tried to explain all this to him?'

'Time and time again, but he doesn't understand. I've no choice, Amalia, I've got to go home. I've thought and thought about it until I can't think any more.'

Her voice rose, and Francisco started to whimper. Instantly Amalia leant over the bed and rocked the crib. 'Hush, my little darling. Hush, my precious.' The bird-like noise subsided and she straightened up.

'I still think you're wrong, Lorna. I know I said you shouldn't expect people to change, but when you are married you alter without realizing it. You find yourself accepting something you would never have swallowed when you were single.' She looked down at her hands. 'If anyone had told me I'd take my husband back knowing he'd had a mistress I'd have said they were crazy!'

'Good heavens – you knew?'

'He didn't try very hard to keep it a secret.' Amalia's lips quivered. 'You love Rafael because he's strong and I love Manoel because he's weak. The only difference is that I'm prepared to make the best of things and you're unwilling to accept Rafael's strength and everything it entails. In that case I agree you'd be wise to take my aunt's advice and go home. You can't have two dominant partners in a marriage.'

'If only I—'

The rest of Lorna's words were drowned by Francisco's renewed whimpering, and further conversation was lost as the baby began to cry in earnest.

Lorna did not see Amalia again before she left Estoril. She spent the long day packing and sorting her things, unable to restrain bitter tears as she put away the yellow frock. 'Like a candle,' Rafael had described her in it. 'Pure and cold yet burning to the touch.'

'Oh, Rafael,' she cried, 'will I never be able to forget the things you said and the hours we shared? Oh, darling,

darling, I'll never be able to stop loving you as long as I live!'

She would have given everything she possessed not to go down to dinner that evening, but she refused to give the Senhora the pleasure of knowing how she felt, and she defiantly put on a fresh dress and reddened her lips before taking her place at the dining-room table.

The Senhora herself broached the subject of the previous night's discussion. 'I hope you were not too upset by all I said last night, Lorna?'

'You could hardly expect me to be unmoved, when you've ...' her voice trembled, 'when you've destroyed something that could have made my happiness.'

'I could not destroy something that was impregnable. If you had been sure of your love for my son and of my son's love for you, nothing I said would have shaken your faith or happiness. It is because I—'

'Please, senhora, not again.' Lorna pushed back her chair. 'I can't bear any more discussion. You might like to know that I'm leaving in a few hours.'

The old lady's eyebrows raised, but she said nothing as Lorna continued: 'We needn't go into the whys and wherefores. I'm not going to leave a letter for Rafael. There is nothing I can say that can make him understand. I leave it to you to tell him what you see fit.' She twisted off her engagement ring and put it on the table. 'Please give this back to him for me.' She walked to the door. 'It'll probably have to be made smaller for Inez, but I'm sure it can be done!'

At five o'clock the following morning Lorna boarded the *Fernandez* and as the sun rose in the heavens the coastline of Portugal receded farther and farther into the distance.

On the afternoon of the third day they reached Tilbury, and as the grey huddle of sheds and wharves loomed ahead, tears spilled down Lorna's cheeks. What a different homecoming this was from the one she had

envisaged! She had looked forward to returning with
Rafael by her side, to be able to show him her old home,
the countryside she loved and the London streets that
breathed their own air of stolidity. Now she was on her
own with nothing to look forward to except a future
bereft of the man she loved. She gripped the railing in
front of her and concentrated on the tiny, ant-like
creatures who scurried about on the quayside.

She had wired her aunt the bare facts of her arrival
and was gratified to glimpse the familiar squat figure
through the barriers of the Customs shed. In a few
minutes Lorna was clasped in her arms and after one
look at her niece's face Marion Fairfax bundled her into
a taxi.

'How cold it is here,' Lorna shivered and glanced out
at the pavements glistening with rain.

'I expect it's still summer in Portugal.'

'Not quite, but it's much warmer than this. It's so
bleak here, so grey and — and—' she could not go on and
turned her head away. They finished the rest of the
journey in silence, and it was not until they were sitting
over a cup of tea in the kitchen that Lorna recounted the
reasons for her return.

The older woman listened in silence, but as her niece
finished speaking she could not restrain an exclamation
of disgust. 'You're mad! Utterly mad! I'm surprised at
you for not having any more sense than to listen to a
jealous old woman.'

'She's not jealous,' Lorna protested.

'Of course she is. It stands out a mile! I'd an idea something was wrong from the tone of your letters. For a girl
in love you seemed too concerned about customs and
beliefs and the whole ridiculous fandangle of nonsense.
Seems to me your attack of sunstroke left you a bit weak
in the head! Don't you know that nothing's important
except you and Rafael? And if you love him and he loves
you, to hell with everyone else!'

'It isn't always as easy as that. Perhaps if you'd been with me I might have seen things differently. But on my own—'

'That was half the trouble – you were too much on your own! I'd have thought Amalia would have more sense than to let you turn tail and run. What did she say when you told her you were going?'

'The usual things, except that she wasn't quite as vehement in her disagreement as you. She had an idea things weren't working out too well.'

'I see. And what do you think that young man of yours is going to say when he gets home and finds you've gone?'

Lorna stood up. 'I don't know and I don't care! I don't care about him in the least.'

And on this last remark she burst into tears and flung herself weeping into her aunt's arms.

CHAPTER ELEVEN

During the following weeks the numbness that had first protected Lorna began to dissipate and the realization of what she had forfeited by her action was borne in on her. What had Rafael felt when he returned home to find her gone? Time and again she picked up a pen to write and explain why she had run away, but always at the last moment her courage failed her. How could she explain in a letter what she had never been able to express by word? No, there was nothing she could do. She had run away, and the next move was up to him. Anxiously she scanned the post to see if there was a letter from him; every time the telephone rang her pulses jumped. But the weeks passed without a word or a sign of his love, and gradually pride superseded any other emotion. Yet what had she expected him to do? Remembering the market at Cascais she heard his voice as he guided her to the old man's stall. 'We Portuguese are a proud race,' he had said. She should have remembered that before it was too late.

Slowly Lorna began to pick up the threads of life again. She telephoned her friends and told them she was back. Luckily she had only written to her aunt and Derek of her engagement, and though one or two of the girls hinted at a romance Lorna made no mention of it and merely said that she had found herself homesick for grey skies and rain! She started to look for a new job and decided to find something entirely different from her last post at the hotel. She wanted to do nothing that reminded her of Rafael. Her life was beginning anew and this time everything must be different.

It was Derek who finally sent her along to see a Mr. Browning of Browning, Murray and Sons, Solicitors, and although the building she entered was far less pretentious than the Hyde Park Palace Hotel, the job appeared to be much more absorbing and rewarding.

Mr. Browning dealt with the conveyancing side of the practice, but because of a weak heart he now found it necessary to have a secretary who would take an active part in helping him to decide which estates or similar properties should come under his jurisdiction.

Lorna quickly adapted herself to her new job. She had to travel a great deal and was frequently away from London visiting remote places in Berkshire, Warwickshire and Northumberland. Travelling round the countryside she knew more than ever how impossible it would have been to have given up her homeland. The luminous green of the grass might not compare favourably with the lush meadows of southern Portugal, nor could the bays and inlets of Devon or Cornwall, with its red-gold sand and rough grey sea, compare with the glowing Praia da Rocha or Serra d'Arribada, yet it meant so much more to her. Difficult to believe that the ties of home could be so strong.

Occasionally she wondered whether Derek had purposely recommended her to this job, whether he had hoped that by strengthening her love of the countryside he would accentuate the difference between her and Rafael. If that had been his intention he was only succeeding in part, for although in her journeyings she grew to love England more, she also found herself wondering what compensation there was in the landscape that could compare with Rafael's kisses and the tender strength of his arms.

The time flew by, Christmas was nearly here, and before she knew it her birthday loomed ahead. Derek invited her to a dinner-dance to celebrate, but she refused.

'Aunt Marion wants to give a party for me and I can't disappoint her. There'll only be a few people, but it should be fun.'

'I'm sure it will,' Derek said stiffly. 'You needn't tell me how popular you are.'

'I didn't mean that at all! If you want to pick a quarrel . . .'

'I don't.' He caught her hand. 'But you can't blame me for being jealous. Ever since you've come back you've held me at arm's length. You've altered, Lorna. You've made more friends in the last few months than you've ever had before.'

'You should be pleased. Don't you want me to have any friends?'

'Of course, but – damn it, Lorna, you're different, that's all.'

Stirred at the perplexity in his voice, she put her hand on his arm. 'I haven't changed fundamentally, Derek. I know I'm not the same girl who went away six months ago, but then everybody alters.'

'I don't mind you altering,' he said fiercely, 'as long as you don't leave me behind in the process.' She said nothing and he continued: 'You've never told me why you broke your engagement to Rodriguez and I don't want to know, but I took it to mean that you've finished with him. I can't offer you as much as he could, but at least we both think alike and I love you with all my heart.'

'Derek, I—'

'Please, Lorna, let me finish. I know you're not in love with me. That's what you were going to say, weren't you? Well, it doesn't matter. I've got enough love for two of us, and once we're married you'll forget Rodriguez. I'll *make* you forget him. Please, Lorna, say you'll marry me.'

'I don't – I can't!' She turned and stared blindly out of the window. 'I know you've never spoken about Rafael, and – and thank you for not asking any questions. You've been awfully patient and sweet, but at the moment I can't think of marrying anyone. It's too soon.'

'Nearly three months.' He moved to her side and put his hands on her shoulders, drawing her towards him.

She tensed nervously in his arms, but did not move away.

'Three months,' he repeated. 'It's a long time, Lorna. Long enough for you to know that he's not going to follow you. I've given him his chance, but he's not taken it, and now it's up to me. I can't put what I feel for you into flowery words, but I love you just as deeply as – as anyone else. I want you to marry me, Lorna, and you can't expect me to wait for ever.'

Although the matter was left in abeyance Lorna knew she could not postpone her decision much longer, and her approaching birthday was coloured by the knowledge that this was the day Derek would choose for his reply. She longed to refuse him, but her sincere fondness for him and her aunt's assertion that no woman was truly happy living alone made her hesitate. Perhaps it would be best to accept Derek after all. Surely in making him happy she would find some contentment too?

In an effort to forget that she would soon be committing herself to a man she did not love, Lorna threw herself into the preparations for her party. The furniture was moved from the living-room and the carpets turned back to leave a small square for dancing. The family silver was taken out and polished and the kitchen piled high with delicately cut sandwiches, gateaux, and a large birthday cake in the shape of a question mark.

As there was still so much preparation to do for the party Lorna asked Mr. Browning if she could leave early, and he readily agreed.

Lorna arrived at the flat to find her aunt rushing excitedly from one room to the other. She started to help to carry in the dishes and drinks, pretending to a light-heartedness she did not feel. She stood for a moment in the hall wondering where she would have spent her birthday if she had not run away from Portugal: in some strange land on a terrace under palm trees, being toasted across a table for two, Rafael's eyes warm and tender as he raised his glass.

'Don't stand there dreaming,' her aunt said severely. 'Come down to earth.'

'Sorry, darling. What do you want me to do?'

'Nothing, everything's ready. Go and change or you'll be late.'

Lorna went up to her room and stopped in surprise at the magnificent spray of pale green orchids on the bed. The card attached was from Derek, and with a little sigh she unclipped it and placed the blooms on the dressing-table. Each petal curled into the next, the delicate fronds speckled with gold, shading to pink at the heart. They brought the garden at Estoril vividly to mind and she had only to close her eyes to see the riot of blooms that bordered the long green lawns, the exquisite flowers and plants that opened to the blazing sun. She shook her head and firmly brought her mind back to the present. In half an hour her guests would be arriving and unless she hurried she would be late.

In honour of the occasion she had bought a dress of ruby red velvet, trimmed with soft white fur. Skilful use of cosmetics could transform any Cinderella into a princess, she thought ironically some fifteen minutes later, for the delicately made up sophisticate that stared back at her in no way resembled the wan, unhappy-looking girl who had come into the room earlier. She turned from her appraisal as her aunt came into the room with a letter.

'I forgot to give you this, it came today from Portugal.'

Lorna took the letter with trembling hands, her pulses showing as she recognized Amalia's writing. Carefully she opened it and began to read.

'My Dearest Lorna,

This is just to tell you that Manoel and I are leaving for Brazil tomorrow with Francisco and Nannie, a dragon of a Scotswoman whom Rafael found for us (trust him!).

I'm sorry my letters have been so brief since you left, but I haven't had much time since I came from the nursing home. Now, with all our trunks packed and nothing to do until we leave tomorrow, I really feel I must sit down and say hello to you all over again.

You will not be surprised to hear that Rosalia is now Deveer. Although the wedding was a simple one there was a great hullabaloo about it, and your eyes would have popped out if you had seen the linens and silver in her trousseau! This house was so full of family I could have screamed, but thank goodness most of them have already left.

Inez was a bridesmaid, and although I don't like her I must say she looked beautiful. She's still here and struts around like the cat that swallowed the canary, in this case the canary being Rafael.'

At this point Lorna's legs gave way and she sat down on the edge of the bed. Although she had imagined the eventuality of Rafael getting married, seeing it confirmed was like reading her own epitaph. She bent her head to the letter again, tears blurring the print.

'I don't know how you feel now you are home again, Lorna. Your letters have been so noncommittal that I can't read between the lines, but I suppose you want it this way. I didn't know whether or not to mention Rafael's name or to tell you that Inez was here, but if we're going to keep in touch in the future I don't want to hide things from you now. Don't keep me waiting too long for a letter, I'm dying to know whether you see much of Derek and if any romance is brewing between you.

I've never thanked you properly for coming out here to keep me company. It was like old times having you with me and I hope we won't have to wait years before meeting again.

Now I really must stop. Manoel's waiting to take me out and he's getting impatient. Believe it or not, he's been most attentive since I've come home, and I intend to keep him up to scratch!'

The rest was an almost illegible scrawl with the signature standing out clearly.

Slowly Lorna put down the letter and stood up. If she had been in any doubt about her future course, Amalia's letter had more than shown her the way. How easily Rafael had forgotten her; how quickly Inez had been restored to favour! Well, she had learned her lesson, and if the sun never shone quite as brightly for her, or the beauty of the moon seem quite as appealing, no one except herself would know.

Soon the party was in full swing, and flitting from one person to the other Lorna had little time to think. The radiogram played softly and a few couples began to dance while others laughed and talked, their voices raised against the clinking of glasses and music.

Derek was the last to arrive, and Lorna greeted him warmly.

'The flowers were marvellous, but you shouldn't have been so extravagant.'

'You invite extravagance, my pet.' He kissed her lightly. 'Happy birthday, darling, I'm sorry I'm the last to wish it to you.' He took off his coat. 'Never be an accountant, my dear, I'm so busy worrying about other people I haven't time to worry about myself.'

'That's just as well.' She led him into the room and waved her arm. 'I think you know most of the people, so I won't bother to introduce you.'

'And those I don't call "bud". I'm sure they'll be only too pleased to answer — especially if I'm offering them a drink!'

In the laughter that followed they moved into the dining-room and Lorna was kept busy passing plates of sandwiches and cakes. It was nearly ten when her aunt appeared from the kitchen with a magnum of champagne.

'A toast to Lorna's birthday!' Derek called. 'Come along folks, fill 'em up!' With a loud pop the cork flew off and champagne frothed into the glasses.

'Speech, Lorna, speech!' someone called.

Lorna looked round the small room. 'I don't know what to say,' she stammered. 'I rehearsed something, but now I've forgotten every word! I'm not awfully good at making speeches, but I'd – like to thank you for coming here and – and—' The door bell rang.

'Saved by the bell!' Derek cried.

'I'll take it,' Marion Fairfax said. 'It might be one of the tenants complaining about the noise.'

'Bring him in and give him a drink. That'll cure his complaints!'

There was more laughter, and as it subsided Marion Fairfax came back.

'A visitor for you, Lorna.'

Lorna took a step forward, drawing back as she saw the tall dark man framed in the doorway. Rafael! The blood pounded in her ears and her body trembled so violently that she could not walk.

'I hope I'm not intruding.' He came towards her, his tan startling by contrast with the unfamiliar dark suit. 'I didn't know you were having a party, Lorna.'

'I – I – it's my birthday.'

'I see. I'd have brought you a present if I'd known.'

'Oh no, there was no need.'

He continued to look at her, and awkwardly she began to introduce him. This done, she looked for Derek, but he was nowhere to be seen, and as Rafael remained firmly by her side she desperately made conversation. 'You must be hungry. Would you like something to eat?'

'No, thank you. I've already dined.'

'A drink, then. You must have a drink.'

She hurried across to the improvised bar and as she turned round with a glass, found that he had followed her. Her hand shook, spilling the liquid, but he took it from her without a word.

'To you, Lorna. A happy birthday.'

'Thank you.' There was a little silence and she searched her mind again for something to say. 'How is everyone? I heard from Amalia today and she told me she was leaving for Brazil. Rosalia's married, isn't she? It must be quiet in the house now, apart from your mother, I mean. I – I—'

Still he said nothing, and she continued: 'I didn't know you were in England. How long have you been here?'

'Just over a week.'

'So long?' It was an involuntary exclamation.

'Not long when you consider the business I had to do. I came to see you at the first opportunity.'

'There was no need,' she said hastily. 'Now if you'll excuse me – the other guests . . .'

Not for anything in the world could she have remained at his side a moment longer! Why had he chosen today of all days to arrive? Indeed, why had he bothered to come at all? With grim determination she laughed and chattered with her friends, but she was tense to the point of screaming, and with every fibre of her being longed to be alone. Although she did not look at Rafael she was acutely aware of him in the corner of the room, his face aloof and unsmiling as he watched her.

She ignored her aunt's signals to include him in the conversation, but she had reckoned without his magnetic charm and soon he was the centre of attraction, the men amused by his witty conversation, the women by his attentiveness. Only Lorna still held aloof, and she was drained to the point of exhaustion by the time the party started to break up. Slowly the flat emptied until only one of the girls, Derek and Rafael were left.

Betty Sands looked in the direction of the intriguing foreigner and lowered her eyes engagingly.

'It was wonderful to meet you, Senhor Rodriguez.' Her Portuguese pronunciation was atrocious, but she was pretty enough for it not to matter.

Rafael's teeth flashed in a smile. 'The pleasure was all mine.'

'Not at all,' Betty smiled, showing two dimples. 'I hope we meet again. Well, I suppose I'd better be running along, Lorna. It's awfully late, I do hope I can get a taxi.' She looked coyly at Rafael, but he said nothing and there was an awkward silence until Derek bridged the gap.

'Don't worry about a taxi, Betty. I'll take you home.'

'There's no need for you to go,' Lorna said hurriedly. 'We can always get a radio cab. Stay a little while longer.'

' 'Fraid not. I've a busy day ahead and it's past twelve.' Derek moved into the hall and Lorna followed him.

'For heaven's sake don't leave me alone! Can't you see I don't want you to go?'

'I can see a lot of things. That's why I'm not staying. I can't fight your battles, Lorna darling, especially when you don't want to win.'

Before she had a chance to reply Betty came back with her coat and with a last flurry of good-byes Lorna was left alone in the hall.

Marion Fairfax came through from the kitchen with a tea-towel in her hand. 'Thank goodness it's over! I'll just stack some of the glasses in the kitchen.'

'You can't leave me too,' Lorna whispered furiously. 'What is this – a conspiracy?'

'Rubbish! What's the matter with you? You've been pining to see him ever since you got back from Portugal, and now he's here you act as if he were the last man in the world you want to see.'

'I can change my mind, can't I?' Angry tears welled into Lorna's eyes. 'I don't want to have anything to do with him, can't you understand?'

'You're acting like a child. For goodness' sake behave yourself.'

The kitchen door closed, leaving Lorna with no alternative but to return to the drawing-room alone. Her mouth was dry and waves of panic surged up inside her so that she felt physically sick and longed to run out of the flat into the dark streets – anywhere as long as she did not have to face Rafael.

She clenched her hands and closed her eyes, opening them again to find him staring at her.

'Are you ill?' He took a step forward and she drew back.

'No, just tired. It's late and I've had a busy day. Can I get your coat?'

'No, you can't. I didn't come here to be fobbed off with an excuse.' He caught her arm in a painful grip. 'Come inside and sit down. I want to talk to you.'

His voice was cold and distant, and not daring to look at him, she obeyed. For a moment he stared at her bent head.

'My God!' he burst out abruptly. 'The last thing I expected to find was a woman made of ice. How can you sit there looking so calm? Anyone would think we'd never met!' His voice shook with anger. 'You deserve a damn good smack, and I've a good mind to administer it!'

'You're not in Portugal now!' She lifted her head furiously, but as their eyes met her anger evaporated. 'Please go, Rafael,' she whispered, 'please go.'

'Not until I've finished what I want to say.'

'Don't you think you've said enough?'

'I do not! We've got to talk this thing out.'

'No, no, not again! I can't bear it, Rafael.'

'And do you think I can? Do you think that I'm made of stone. *Porra!* How do you think I felt when I got home and found you'd gone? Why didn't you wait to see me? Why did you take the coward's way out?'

'It was the only way. What good would it have done if

we'd seen one another — what good is it doing now? More quarrels, more bitterness.' She turned her back on him and wiped her eyes. 'I wish you'd go,' she said wearily. 'Nothing has changed.'

'On the contrary, a great deal has changed. Unless you do not consider my living in London a matter of interest to you.'

Lorna stared at him incredulously. 'I don't understand.'

'Don't you? It's quite simple. I've transferred my office from Lisbon to London in the short space of three months.'

'You're joking!'

'I do not consider it a joke to give up my home and try to find one of comparable beauty in this city of yours!'

Lorna leant back against the chair. After the excitement of the party and Rafael's appearance, it was too much to learn that he had left Lisbon in order to live in London. She closed her eyes to hide the sudden flow of tears, opening them again as he placed a glass against her lips and forced her to drink. The neat spirit ran down her throat and she choked.

'No, Rafael, I'm all right now.' She pushed the glass away and sat up. 'What you just said — could you repeat it again?'

'I don't want to waste time in words,' he said savagely. 'We've wasted too much time already. The house at Hampton Court will be completely furnished by the end of the month and I can say good riddance to living in a hotel!'

'But why have you left Portugal?'

'Do I need to tell you? You were never stupid, *cara*, except where I was concerned.' He leaned down and tilted her face so that her eyes looked directly into his. 'It's so simple when you think it out. You won't live with me in Portugal, so I must live with you here. You didn't think I was going to let you walk out of my life as easily as all that, did you?' He shook his head. 'Lorna, Lorna, I'm surprised at you. I thought you knew me better than that.'

'But you never wrote – never got in touch with me.'

'There was nothing to say. As you said yourself before, it had all been said. Besides, words wouldn't have convinced you. You wanted action and you've got it.'

She started to laugh, laughed until the tears came into her eyes, and he pulled her into his arms and let her cry against his shoulder.

'I don't know what to say, Rafael, I can't believe it! These last three months have been agony – agony! I couldn't get you out of my mind – couldn't believe I'd never see you again! Oh, darling, if only you'd told me what you were going to do I'd never have let you!' Between her sobs the words tumbled out. 'To think that you're willing to give up your home for me – to say good-bye to your friends and all the things you love. Oh, Rafael, you make me feel such a beast!'

'Do not call the woman I love a beast,' he said sternly. 'She is a darling, an angel, even though she's also a silly, frightened girl.' He took out his handkerchief and tenderly wiped her tears away. 'Don't you know that I love you too much to let anything come between us?'

She leaned back and looked into his face. 'But won't it be difficult for you to live here – for your business, I mean?'

'Fortunately not. I've an office in London anyway, so all it meant was that I've taken my manager's place here and put him into the Lisbon office instead.'

'I can't believe it's so easy.'

'Not easy,' he said ironically, 'but very easy compared to living my life without you.'

She sighed tremulously, and with the tips of her fingers caressed his cheek. 'How did you know I wouldn't have fallen in love with someone else in the last three months?'

His eyes narrowed into tiny pinpoints of light. 'You wouldn't have been the Lorna I knew if you had, and then it would have served me right for misjudging you.'

She was shaken with laughter. 'Oh, darling, you're incorrigible. I'll never be able to fathom the way your mind works!'

'All the better. I want to keep *some* secrets from you!'.

He reached into his pocket and drawing out a familiar leather box removed the ring and slipped it on her finger.

'You once said you'd never put it on a third time,' she said as she looked down at it.

'Because I was stupid and arrogant. But I've learnt enough now to know that you can't have real love without humility.' He stroked back the hair from her temples and kissed the shadows beneath her eyes. 'Darling Lorna, I'm afraid I won't be an easy person to live with. No matter how much I try there'll be times when I'll unwittingly hurt you, when I'll make you cry.'

'Now you're saying things against the man I love!' She twined her arms around his neck, loving the feel of his crisp hair beneath her hands. 'I still can't believe it's true! Are you sure I won't wake up and find I'm dreaming?'

'Will this prove it?'

Her reply was stifled as his mouth came down on hers. Freely she gave herself to his desire, revelling in the knowledge that she could arouse him to a passion that was his master. After a long moment he drew away, shaking his head slightly as he looked down at her parted lips, her half closed eyes.

'I'll have to call you Lorelei if you tempt me like this,' he said huskily.

'Don't you like it?'

'Too much.'

With a happy sigh she relaxed against him. 'I still can't believe you've given up your home for me.'

'Not given it up, *querida*, only left it for a little while. It will be there waiting for us, waiting until our love is cemented by years of happiness and we are so much a part of one another that nothing can come between us — nothing can destroy us! We will go back to Portugal one day, *cara*, but until that time I am willing to live your kind of life.'

'And yet I never said that to you,' she cried. 'You make me feel ashamed. Oh, Rafael, I've been so stupid, I should have known from the first that wherever we are it doesn't matter as long as we're together. I am home when you hold me in your arms, home when you kiss me and say I'm yours.'

'Then you are home for ever,' he whispered against her mouth. 'For ever and ever.'

FREE! Harlequin Romance Catalogue

Here is a wonderful opportunity to read many of the Harlequin Romances you may have missed.

The HARLEQUIN ROMANCE CATALOGUE lists hundreds of titles which possibly are no longer available at your local bookseller. To receive your copy, just fill out the coupon below, mail it to us, and we'll rush your catalogue to you!

Following this page you'll find a sampling of a few of the Harlequin Romances listed in the catalogue. Should you wish to order any of these immediately, kindly check the titles desired and mail with coupon.

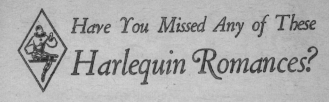

Have You Missed Any of These
Harlequin Romances?

All books are 60c. Please use the handy order coupon.

GG

Have You Missed Any of These
Harlequin Romances?

All books are 60c. Please use the handy order coupon.

HH

Have You Missed Any of These

Harlequin Romances?

All books are 60c. Please use the handy order coupon.